THREE MARYS

OTHER BOOKS BY PAUL PARK

Available from Cosmos Books:
If Lions Could Speak and Other Stories

Available as e-books from ElectricStory.com:
Soldiers of Paradise
Sugar Rain
The Cult of Loving Kindness

Coelestis
The Gospel of Corax

THREE MARYS

PAUL PARK

COSMOS BOOKS

THREE MARYS

Copyright © 2003 by Paul Park

Cover painting "Repentant Magdalene" by George de la Tour
Cover design copyright © 2003 by Garry Nurrish

All rights reserved. No part of this publication may be reproduced or transmitted in any form or by any means, electronic or mechanical, including photocopy, recording, or any information storage and retrieval system now known or invented, without permission in writing from the publisher, except by a reviewer who wishes to quote brief passages in connection with a review written for inclusion in a magazine, newspaper, broadcast, etc.

Published by Cosmos Books, a division of Wildside Press
www.cosmos-books.com, www.wildsidepress.com

Hardcover ISBN: 1-58715-519-2
Paperback ISBN: 1-58715-520-6

A man might think, "Since the House of Shammai declares unclean and the House of Hillel clean, this one prohibits and that one permits, why should I henceforward learn Torah?"

Scripture says, "Words . . . the words . . . these are the words . . . " All the words have been given by a single Shepherd . . . So you build many chambers in your heart and bring into it the words of the House of Shammai and the words of the House of Hillel, the words of those who declare unclean and the words of those who declare clean.

—Tosefta Sotah, 7, 12

For Deborah Brothers
Dear wife, Mariologist

AUTHOR'S NOTE:

I imagine this book's ideal reader will possess two qualities that don't always go together. The first is a working knowledge of the stories of the New Testament, and the second is a willingness to hear those stories retold in unfamiliar ways. In writing this book, it has been my hope that these new points of view might combine with the original texts in the reader's mind, and not deny or contradict them.

CHAPTER ONE:
THE VIRGIN OF MAGDALA

When you say she is possessed with seven devils, this is what you mean. First, she has the falling sickness. Second, she has dreams from the unreal world. Third, she speaks to angels and the spirits of the dead. Fourth, she knows God's laws weren't made for her. Fifth, she has the wandering eye, which gives bad luck. Sixth, she's often tempted toward evil deeds. Seventh, her beauty forces men to look at her. Sometimes they and others tell cruel lies.

You might find these things a burden, but she bears it lightly. Her husband made her strong. She remembers seeing him for the first time when she came to herself in the market at Capernaum, surrounded by the people who had watched her fall.

It was the worst heat of the worst days. She lay on her back with her leg bent under her. He knelt above her with his fingers in her mouth. She tried to bite him. But he was searching for her tongue until he held it between his fingers. All the time he was talking in words she didn't recognize, meaningless soft words, though he was frowning. "Shoor," he said. "Shoor, shoor," and then something else. Later she asked him what the words meant, wondering if he'd used some foreign spell. He laughed. It was the language boys speak on the hillside, talking to the sheep.

What was she doing there that day with her empty basket? She was fourteen years old. She saw a man's dark head with the sun behind it as he knelt above her in the dust. Maybe that sun burned a part of her away. It was hard for her to think about the time gone by.

But people tell her about the house where she grew up. She listens and the words make pictures. Would the pictures come without the words? Her mind is full of things not usual in women: Greek stories, Greek letters, and the names of plants. Songs and dances. In her mind she can catch sight of her father's face as he speaks with his mouth full.

You who are not possessed by devils, maybe you have time to think. But she came to herself in the dirty street with a crowd of men surrounding her. The hot sun in her eyes. Her body slippery with sweat, and one big, bearded stranger with his fingers in her mouth, talking the language of goats. She bit him, and she could feel the muscles of her jaw, the muscles of her neck sore and stiff. Her leg was shaking. The sun was so bright it was black, so hot it was cold. The blood tasted like metal in her mouth.

That's one day she will not forget. And another like it when he married her in Cana after the harvest time. He said he couldn't go without her to where he was going. He looked for her and found her in another town, and brought her to his student's house. He married her according to the customs of the country people. Even in spite of what he told his students, sometimes he imagined a small house and his own garden, where they'd grow old. Or at least he spoke of it once, and then he stopped.

His mother laughed. "What money did you pay? Did she come from Magdala like this?" But he made a canopy out of willow branches. They sat under it together, surrounded by his family and others. His face was red from nervousness. He wouldn't look at her. Later he brought her to a room above the stable where they had broken a pomegranate on the floor. She remembers that, stepping on the slippery seeds with her bare feet, bending over the couch, her dress around her armpits while he had her like a dog. He knew nothing except what he had seen from animals. But she was happy. Sun came through the small window, though the shutter was closed. The stripes lay across her shoulder, across her stomach as she turned over on the couch. He filled her again, then lay asleep. She lay with her fingers in his hair, feeling the cramps, the soreness of her body. As he slept, something burst in her, a trickle of monthly blood which dripped along the inside of her thigh.

She heard the animals snuffling in their pens. Outside in the garden the guests were calling for wine, cursing the servants because there wasn't any more. She heard his mother's voice. Jeshua didn't stir. Later she got to her feet and stood in her dress next to the shutter, looking down through the slats. As she stood there, a drop of blood fell to the floor, and then another.

The couch had been made up for them. She took one of the linen cloths to bind herself. There was enough blood for him to boast of her virginity. With one foot on the couch, she held a handful of linen under her dress. She was light-headed, sick from cramping. She listened to the animals below her, the voices in the yard. She imagined her blood dripping through the cracks in the floor, spotting the backs of the cows in their pens. And if there were men sleeping drunken in the straw, spotting their upturned cheeks. She imagined traces of her blood borne on the air, a small current of air. Outside in the yard there were six stone water pots set for the men to wash themselves. She imagined specks of blood borne on the wind, dropping down into the stone pots. She imagined the water made red, so they could drink and be purified and their voices would be silent as the sun went down and the darkness gathered in the stifling air.

This was the first of her husband's mighty works, which she will set down later so that everyone will know how he changed water into wine. The last of his works was on the day of his death. In the afternoon they crucified him.

Now she kneels on Golgotha under the gallows tree. And though she can't look at him, still she knows what he is saying. She hears his voice inside her head. "I thirst." Later, "God, my strength, you've let me go." Then, "It is finished," and the world will change, though not at once. She hears a ringing in her ears. She falls forward to her hands and knees and feels the small stones scrape her wrists, hurt her palms. The white hill is blotted out. She lets her head fall until her forehead touches the dust. Later she will see in her mind's eye the history of that hour, which will be confirmed by other witnesses. She'll say she stood in the tabernacle where no woman had ever been. She saw the curtain of Solomon slide apart from its own weight, in that temple of corrupt and fornicating priests.

She'll say she stood in the Kidron valley by the tomb of Absalom, and she felt the earth groan apart. Or in the street of the cheese makers, she saw a donkey kick a lamp into a pile of straw in his stable underneath the house. That fire burned for two days.

But now she's kneeling in the dust at Golgotha, and Jeshua is dead. His mother and his mother's cousin Salome are huddled near her in the rocks. And the girl, Simon the leper's daughter, whom the men call Cleopas's whore.

Some men have come up from the city now the soldiers have gone back. They stand talking with Jeshua's mother. Beyond them the sun is sinking into the red dust.

All morning and all afternoon she stood or knelt among the rocks. But she didn't look. With her eyes pushed shut she listened to the voices of the soldiers, the clatter of the wooden beams, the blows of the hammer and the men screaming and whimpering. Or else she looked at the white stones in front of her, round and perfect as eyes. Or she studied the trunks of the gallows trees, rough and splintered where they disappear among the rocks. A crowd of men were crucified that day.

But now she raises herself up. Nor does she spare herself. She looks into the thicket of trees. She finds Jeshua, and she can see he didn't suffer. God took him before he suffered, she tells herself. At that moment she forgets her anger, though she can't forgive him. He died out of his own stubbornness. Nor did he say goodbye, but sat talking as Thomas Didymus led her away. Didn't he see her go? No, because already he'd left her time and time again, so that dirty men like Simon the leper thought she was his whore and not his wife. Why should she mourn him when he'd treated her like that? Why did he rob her of her grief, so she has to share it with these women?

"You stop crying now," says Jeshua's mother. "Come here."

She is with two of her younger sons, Joses and Simon, and two old men. Salome is there, and Simon the leper's daughter, and a black girl, a slave.

"We've got work to do," says Jeshua's mother. She's a big, ugly woman. Her neck is spotted and thin. Her voice is rough.

Mary of Magdala stumbles toward them. Her knees are sore and bruised. She feels stupid and light-headed, and it takes some minutes of listening for her to understand what they are saying to each other.

But it is plain. They mean to take her husband down and bury him according to the law.

Why is she not part of these decisions? Blinking, she looks around. The soldiers have returned to the Antonia, but three are left.

They live in a house among the rocks. Two have gone down with the ladders and ropes, but one still stays, walking with his spear among the gallows trees.

"It's just an alcove in the tomb, but he says it's not been used. I had to pay him the money," says the old woman, Jeshua's mother. She's talking about the thirty silver pieces, which later she will say she got from Claudia Procula, Pilate's wife.

"All of it?" asks Joses.

The sun is setting now. Except for their small group, everyone is gone now from the hill. They are frightened of the coming dark. An old man and an old woman climb down through the rocks, but they're the last.

From the city comes the sound of horns, because the sabbath is beginning. The dry hills have been silent, waiting, but now they are full of small noises, because the feast has come. In the houses below Golgotha, people are lighting lamps.

"Did anyone speak for him?" asks red-faced Salome. She is carrying a basket.

One of the old men shakes his head. "Joanna's husband talked to Caiaphas in the council. This was Pilate's choice, not theirs, but they won't mourn him now. They never got anything but curses from him. As for his body, they don't care. They think thirty silver pieces is enough."

"And now it's gone," Joses says. "You should have kept it for a bribe."

His mother shrugs. She nods up the hill. "You can't speak to them.

13

And it's their lives."

She's talking about the soldiers who guard the dead. One of them comes up the hill again to join his friend. They stand watching, not far away.

"I mean thirty drachmae," says Joses. "It's a lot."

"I begged him. I went on my knees." She shrugs. "He was always like that."

She's talking about a relative, a rich man, a camel driver in Jerusalem. He owns land in Arimathea and a tomb north of the city, in a garden off the Joppa road.

Above them the sky is already full of stars. The night will be cold, though there's no wind. The whole year has been cold, Mary thinks. She sits down suddenly on a broken stone. She listens to the sound of someone crying. It makes her sick to hear it, a raw, coughing noise.

She closes her eyes, and in her mind's eye it's bright day. She feels her husband behind her, feels his hands on her shoulders, and he's kissing her on her lips and neck and shoulders. He doesn't speak out loud, for he is kissing her.

But he is there with her, the way he never will be for these others. What does she care what they say? What does she care where his grave will be?

Part of her does care. When she opens her eyes, the two soldiers have moved away beyond the top of the hill. One of the men with Jeshua's mother says, "We'll have to fool them. Or else wait till they fall asleep."

An old ladder lies discarded in the rocks, a hollowed-out tree trunk, quarter-round, with small steps cut into it. The wood is split almost from top to bottom. The lower steps are worn away.

Joses says, "Mother, you must go. These others will go with you to the Joppa road. Make the grave and wait for us. Somebody is there already with a light."

"No," answers the old woman. "I want my son." She rubs her mouth. The soldiers stand among the rocks, watching.

The man who found the ladder has a thin gray beard. "I can think of a distraction," he says. "Send the young one, Cleopas's wife. There's something soldiers understand." Then he laughs, not cruelly.

"Don't call her that," says the old woman. Men obey her when she speaks. "She's a child. She'll go with us to the grave." She puts her arm around the girl. Then she turns and calls to Mary. "Nicodemus will take you back. This is no place for you."

The moon is rising above the silver hills. By its small light Mary of Magdala watches Salome unpack the basket. She unpacks the winding cloth and the soudarion. She unpacks the food and wine. And a sealed pot which she tucks into her dress.

"She ought to come with us," says Salome. "She has a right to be there."

But the old woman shakes her head. "You can't tell what she'll do. We don't have time to lead her like a fool. I'll bring her when the sabbath's done."

Nicodemus is a small, thin man. Already he is moving down the hill. Light-headed, Mary stands up to follow him. And then Salome is pushing the basket into her hands. A jar of wine remains in it and two sweet loaves. "Take this for him," she murmurs, nodding down the hill. "I'm sorry."

Jeshua's mother also has a jar tucked in her dress, and Mary feels it against her stomach as the old woman puts her skinny arms around her. "Don't cry," she says. "I'll be there soon."

She kisses Mary on the shoulder. But then she grabs hold of her wrist as Mary puts her hand into the pot. "What are you doing? This isn't for you."

But it is. It's the ointment for the dead. She brings her hand up to her face and rubs the grease into her cheek. It smells of myrrh and aloes-wood.

"You stop that. Now go." And Mary is stumbling down the dark hill. Her bare feet knock against the stones. She is holding Nicodemus's basket, looking for him, but he hasn't waited. Or he's at the bottom of the hill, waiting on the road.

She stumbles down until she is alone. But then she stops. Above her on the hill beneath the circle of crosses, the two soldiers light a lantern. She turns to look, waits several minutes, but no one comes.

Salome and the old woman were there at Cana when she sat under the canopy. Now they leave her by herself. She waits in the darkness, and after a few minutes she chooses a different way. With the basket on her arm she climbs up toward the gallows. Skirting the hill, she climbs up from the other side.

There's a language soldiers understand, she thinks. In the darkness, the white stones seem to shine. She wraps her shawl around her shoulders, covers her face and head.

Once in her father's house she heard a story which was popular among the Greeks. In Ephesus a widow swore she'd die over her husband's grave. A soldier heard her groans, saw her light among the tombs and went to visit her. He was guarding a man's body. In the morning he went back to the tree, but the body was gone. The man's relatives had come and stolen it for burial. But the widow said, "Take my husband and nail him up. I've lost one man I loved. I won't lose another."

The widow in the story is beautiful. She's black-haired, black-eyed, with a white neck and long hands. Mary sees her now as she picks her way among the stones. And the soldier is behind her, holding her white shoulders in his well-remembered hands.

Weighed down by the basket, Mary stops. The darkness gathers around her. Now she thinks about her husband, how he'd kiss her on her shoulders and her neck. She feels a sudden rush of sickness, and then her ankle twists under her, and she sits down. She sits between two rocks below the crest of the hill, below the hanging body of some murderer or thief. Her husband's gallows is beyond her sight. It is hidden in the darkness. It is on the other side of the circle of crosses that crowns the summit of the hill.

Overcome with sickness, she bows her head and puts the basket between her feet as the tears leak out of her. She rubs her cold bare feet together and then rubs them with her hands.

Then from inside her belt she draws the knife which she bought. She lays it down out of sight in a cleft between two rocks. She sprinkles the dry sand over it. She thinks she hasn't made a sound, but the soldiers hear her. She sits up and puts her hands over her face. With her eyes closed she listens to the rattle of the lantern and the sound of small stones kicked away. Then she opens her eyes and looks into the swinging circle of the light.

It's a lamp in a pierced tin box, hanging at the end of a small chain. By its light she sees the legs of a man, though his head is still in darkness. Golden light picks out the hairs on his legs, the buckle of his sandal.

He puts the lamp down and then squats down so she can see his face. And it's true, the story is true. He is a handsome man a little younger than she, maybe sixteen years old. He has the face of a young boy, a beardless angel, she thinks. He is blue-eyed, golden-haired.

She is crying more than ever, though she doesn't make a sound. He knows. He puts his hand out and then hesitates. He almost touches her with his finger. His face is gentle, sad.

She crosses her arms over her breasts and hugs herself, because she's cold. She feels the gooseflesh on her arms, her breasts. Then she turns her face away. But she still feels his nearness, though he doesn't touch her. She feels his hand near her arm. Then it's gone, and she hears a whispering sound, which is the cloth pulled from the mouth of the basket.

She thinks maybe her shoulders are shaking from her tears. Maybe he doesn't want to disturb her. But then she hears his voice call out, not loud, not to her. Words in a foreign tongue, harsh and strange.

Turned away, her face hidden in her shawl, she doesn't see the second man. But she hears the creak of his knees as he squats down. And she hears them talking, whispering to each other. There's a rustle of soft laughter. Without looking, she can see their faces. She can see the small circles of their beardless lips.

All this time she has been crying. But there's something else inside her too, something she hasn't felt in a long time. Jeshua cured her of the falling sickness. Now he's dead only a few hours, and already she feels the aching in the back of her teeth. Her tongue is restless. Her mouth is full of a sweet liquid which she swallows. She hears them crack the wax seal on the wine jar, and she smells the raw, unfiltered wine.

Then she feels nothing and hears nothing for a while. Her mind is in darkness. But in the middle of the darkness is her husband's voice. "If you die, then you will never die," he says. "A grain of wheat is nothing, unless it dies and falls into the earth."

A light surrounds him, darkens his face and hurts her eyes. But she remembers the strength of his body, and when he holds her now she can't breathe. But her body welcomes him, as it did in the old days. She feels a sweetness, a looseness in her legs. She leans back on the stones.

Still the tears leak out of her. Her body runs with sweat. She leans back against the cold rocks, and then she feels the soldiers pulling at her shawl, loosening it around her neck, pulling it away. She imagines the red cloth damp with tears.

Her eyes are closed, but she knows the men are looking at her. She knows they've raised the lantern to look. She wonders if she should open her eyes. There's an unluckiness in her left eye. Some men care, some don't. Some cross the street to get away from her. But these men are from a land beyond the sea.

Or else they're not men at all, but spirits sent by God to keep her husband's body and her own. Those other men who work in secret on the other side of the hill, who are they? Not friends of hers. Now are they hoisting up the broken ladder? Now is one standing against the gallows while another climbs onto his shoulders? Or perhaps now they're winding the linen cloths around her husband's body. Here on the other side she feels her shawl lifted from her, unwound from her shoulders, her arms. She feels each pebble and sharp stone beneath her. She feels the cold air prickle on her skin. But these soldiers, she imagines the warmth of their bodies. They touch her without touching her, bringing their hands close and then pulling away.

Except there were three soldiers on the hill. Only two are here with her.

She opens her eyes. And she's right: there's no sudden gesture, no word of fear, no curse against bad luck. They look at her and she looks back, unblinking. There's the young man and an older one with heavy brows and a yellow beard. He has a scar on his cheek.

What power brought them to this hill? What power took them from their snowy forests, their cold swamps? Do they have women there who wait for them? The older man is fingering her hair, touching the curls under her ear. The color is unusual among the Jews, but perhaps he's used to it.

They have broken open the wine jar, and the younger one is drinking. The older man is chewing on a cake. He touches her cheek with the side of his knuckle. He touches her lips with his broad thumbnail.

Then he's pulling at her dress, untying her belt and the ribbons at her waist. He searches for the slits in the blue wool and pulls the ribbons out. Her dress parts down the front. He pulls her dress apart to show her linen underclothes, and stops. He brings his hands to his face to touch his own cheeks and lips, whispers something, and then laughs again.

The young man's face is sad as he stares at her. But now the older man is talking constantly, maybe small words of shame and surprise. Or else he's trying to reassure her as he touches her. She wonders if he's one of the men who crucified her husband. Is he touching her with the same hands? If so, they're softer now, fumbling with her linen clothes, untucking them, finding the small ties and then pulling back the cloth. Is he one of the ones that stripped her husband's clothes away as he stood in the Antonia, then sent him out naked to the crowd? She lies back on her elbows as he kneels above her. She lets her head fall back.

Now he strips her belt away and pulls her dress over her legs. He's touching her bare legs. And he's still muttering under his breath. He is on his knees in front of her, holding out his hand. When she does nothing, he reaches down and pulls her upright to her knees. Now her dress falls away from her arms and over her hips, so it lies in a circle around her on the ground. But then he's pulling at her linen clothes, and she imagines for the first time he might strip her naked. She imagines herself naked in front of him, except for the linen cloth around her thighs. But even this cloth she imagines him pulling away until she's as naked as her husband when they nailed him down. No, but she can't, not to save her life or lose it. Is it the custom in the snowy forests for these men to have their women without any shame at all?

Or perhaps it is their shame that keeps them warm. Her cheeks are hot, her skin burns where he touches her. She closes her eyes. Breathing the cold air, she catches the smell of myrrh and aloes-wood, still on her cheek.

Now she wonders where her grave will be. These soldiers, will they bury her to save themselves? Will they leave her for the dogs when they run away? Or surely Jeshua's mother and Salome and the rest will come to look for her. Right now, perhaps, they're winding Jeshua's body in the shroud, rubbing his wounds with perfume, carrying him to Joseph's garden to the tomb they bought for him.

But there are three soldiers on the hill. Only two are here.

She wonders what will become of her clothes, her dress which lies around her. Will they use it to cover her? Jeshua's shirt, which she'd woven in one piece out of white goat's wool—what soldier wears it now?

The older man stops his muttering. He no longer touches her. He is staring at her, and she bows her head. Then she feels soft fingers on her eyes. When she looks up, she sees the younger man. His face is puzzled, sad.

Perhaps the older soldier is the one who crucified her husband. But this one, perhaps he's the spirit God has sent for her. Now she is kneeling as she will before God's chair. Between her knees is the cleft rock and the knife inside it. Does it hurt? she thinks. Does it hurt to die? Or are you so caught up that you can't feel it?

Or if God refuses her, leaves her wandering naked in the darkness, then what can be the difference between this life and that death? Perhaps she's already in the underworld where Hermes and Anubis rule as kings. Perhaps on Golgotha the line is delicate. It won't hurt her to cross over.

Non dolet, she thinks: it doesn't hurt. Then she takes the knife out of the rocks. She raises it above her head, the men flinch away. These things are easily accomplished in the Roman stories. But when she brings the knife into her side, the blade catches in her linen shirt, then twists on the bones of her ribs. It won't go in. The young soldier holds her wrist and cuts himself along his palm. The knife breaks, and the copper blade falls among the stones. The older man gets to his feet, shouting, and at the same time she's conscious of another noise, the sound of her sickness coming out, the shrill wail like the scream of a ghost. Even as she hears it, she wonders whether it is real. Or if she is mimicking it out of a memory. It doesn't matter. She falls onto her face and the scream grows louder all around her. She tastes blood in her mouth.

Stiff and trembling, she feels herself at the top of a tall cliff with the wind and the dark night all around. She feels God tempting her to jump. She asks God for a gift and then she throws herself down. But before she falls into the darkness, she hears the gift come true. She hears a man call from the top of the hill, and then the sound of the third soldier's boots as he comes sliding, stumbling among the rocks.

* * *

At this moment you might judge her harshly, and so do others. On the far side of the hill, Miriam of Nazareth hears the voice of her son's wife. Joses and Simon have the body now. They've pulled it off the tree. But what use now is the tomb she bought in Aceldama? Mary of Magdala knows about it, and she is with the soldiers.

The old woman speaks a curse. There is no time. She speaks a message to the slave girl, sends her down the hill. Joses and Simon stumble with their burden. They were always clumsy.

But Mary of Magdala is incapable of treachery. These moments of surrender when she jumps are the most passionate of her life. When she comes to herself, that night on Golgotha, she imagines lying at the bottom of a pit. The sky is far away. She lies looking at the moon. Then in time, little by little, she imagines herself rising, and the cold sky surrounds her. She lies on the rocks in her linen clothes.

Her side hurts where she has cut herself. Without touching it, she imagines the shallow wound, the blood already hardened and the cloth stuck to it. She listens to a sound come out of her, a wheezing noise. It is the sound that has brought her to herself and brought her up out of the pit, supporting her like an inflated bladder. From the houses below Golgotha she hears the shouts of the feast. On the hill above her she can hear a muffled banging and a loud voice calling in a harsh tongue. Now she's wondering at her stupidness, to think she could die on passover night. No, there was a sacrifice, but it wasn't she. As for these other men who touched her, who nailed up Jeshua of Nazareth, they will be punished. Their centurion will blame them when he finds the body gone.

Perhaps they know already. Beside her hand, the lantern has gone out. But in the moonlight she can see the youngest soldier covered in a blanket, sitting with his knees up and his arms around them, listening to the tiny sounds coming out of her. He lifts his head and she can see his young face, beautiful in the moonlight. She wants to soothe him, make him understand. "He was my husband," she says in the Greek language. Her tongue is swollen, sore.

She imagines he might smile and forgive. Certainly he does nothing to stop her as she sits up, pulls her woolen dress over her shoulders, knots her belt. She looks into his face, and maybe now he sees her wandering eye. He has his hand raised, his five fingers spread, as if pushing off a blow.

She takes the empty basket. Dizzy, she has to rest on her bruised hands and knees. She has to crawl some distance on her hands and knees among the rocks, before she stumbles to her feet and climbs down to the road.

She climbs down to the village below the hill. She thinks it is past midnight of the second watch. Good people are indoors, asleep or with their children. But there are plenty of the others in the poor streets which spread out without pattern from the north wall of Jerusalem. Men have come from Galilee, where the moneylenders have pushed them from their land. Now several families live together in a single room of mud and straw. Or they live in the streets, and for them the sabbath is a time for drunkenness. Men light lamps and put them on the thresholds, just a piece of wick in a clay dish. Sometimes women stand inside the doorway, inside the curtain with the lamp at their feet.

Mary walks down through the roads. In some places the mud walls have collapsed because of the rains. Drunken men call out to her. Women turn away. She wraps her shawl around her face, not that it makes a difference. Men stand in the middle of the street with their arms stretched out. The town is full of country people for the feast. Limping with her empty basket, she pushes past them to the crossroad where the houses give out suddenly in the terraced fields of the landlords. In the moonlight the fields are white with the new grain.

She has a cramp in her right side where she cut herself. She imagines she is grateful for the pain, for her bruised knees and feet, for the cold night. Her mouth is swollen, her teeth ache. Her head aches from her illness. But she imagines herself grateful, because she finds that she can fill her mind with these small things, with the cold dust and the stiffened mud under her bare feet. In time she pulls her shawl down over her shoulders to feel the wind on her face and neck.

Once her father's second wife bought some painted cards. Greeks sold them in the market, pretty things, bright colored portraits, birds, flowers, sometimes household scenes. She and Thamis were almost the same age, and they peeked at them together, wonder-struck, happy to break the law. Several pictures were of naked women in the act of love.

They were painted on a black background in red and silver lines. Now, walking along the road, Mary imagines her own future as a version of the same set. She does it to distract herself, as she welcomes her discomfort. She draws the pictures and fills them with detail, with everything but movement.

These are the pictures she imagines: the high priestess, the slave, the dying queen, the whore, the mad old beggar-woman on the road. A woman sits on the altar step with the veil over her face. Or there is a widow in the house of her new master. Her hair is short, her eyes dark with grief. She kneels at her loom.

The whore is standing inside the curtain of the doorway with the flickering lamp below her at her feet. And then another in the road itself, her face painted, her breasts outlined in red and covered with silk gauze, her hands outstretched. Then another. Mary presses her hand into her side to feel the sticky blood.

Once in her father's house in Magdala before she ran away, she looked down from an upstairs window to see a woman carried through the streets, supported in a litter on the shoulders of four men. Then she thought, "She has no husband." The woman had red hair like her own, tied up in heavy curls around her head. She wore a golden dress.

Now she stops walking. Standing on the road under the stars, she listens to herself sing part of a wordless song, which a slave taught her long before. "Oh my husband," she thinks. All at once she has a memory of him, sitting in his tent, his hand over the lamp—when was it? After they had heard of John's death, that man who had been baptizing in Galilee. Now on that day at the lake, hundreds of John's followers came out of the desert, asking Jeshua of Nazareth to lead them, because he had once been John's disciple. But he sent them home.

She'd loved him then. Simon Peter and the others called him crazy. He stood above the water and scolded those who spoke to him. "John told you to sweat and bleed until God came to deliver you. He told you to count the hours till the world's end. Now he is dead, and Herod lies with his brother's wife, and God is nowhere to be seen."

When they were alone in the tent, he laughed and said he'd tried to feed a thousand people with five loaves of bread. He said Simon Peter and the others wouldn't forgive him, and he laughed.

He sat beside the flickering lamp. The wind made the tent shudder in the night. She had oil in her hands, which she rubbed into his hair and the muscles of his shoulders. "You are my king," she said, and it was true. His big arms shone in the lamplight, wet with oil.

Now, sitting on a cold stone beside the road, she remembers what he said as he was dying. "Ah, my strength, you have forsaken me." It is a verse from David's song. All this time she has been muttering a tune, and now the song comes out of it, soft and true, because her voice also is beautiful, as she can hear and everyone has always said. She sings the words that she remembers: "They push out their lips and shake their heads . . . "

But then the song goes silent, because in the darkness she hears it interrupted from the ditch beside the road, a scratching sound.

She sits on a stone beyond the crossroads. No house is near. She hears a sound which might be from a wild animal that eats the corpses of the crucified.

Now again there's something. Now it's quiet. When she gets to her feet and starts to walk again, she imagines a wild dog moving with her through the darkness, imagines another voice, and she can scarcely understand the words: "But it was you that took me from my mother's womb."

The moonlight shines on the dry mud. She imagines someone walking beside her and a little ahead, in the darkness just beyond her sight. And then in a few minutes it seems as if there really might be someone up ahead, walking with her, hidden in the darkness—"No, who are you?" she says. But she doesn't have to hear his voice. "I will protect you," he says, his voice clear and cold inside her. "This is how. Your husband died because he told lies in God's name. Nor did he love you."

"You are with me from my mother's womb," she says aloud.

When was it, she thinks, that Jeshua stopped loving her? It wasn't all at once. But in time he gave up working in the market, and his mother scolded him because he was her oldest son. He'd spent his boyhood in Sepphoris shaping spoons and wooden cups. Her other sons were fools.

Once he'd worked to feed them, but he wanted to be free of that. Nor did Mary of Magdala blame him to his face. She was used to begging on the roads. But he imagined himself on a high, lonely hill. He made his way among strangers. He had nothing, wanted nothing, but traveled wearily from place to place. The ground hurt his feet. He spoke to people who didn't know him, who cared nothing about what he said.

Would it have been different, she asks herself not for the first time, if God had given her a child?

And if Jeshua had let her stay until the end, she would never have left him like those others. If she'd been at Gesthemene with him that night, the soldiers would have had to drag her away. She would have followed him to the Antonia, even if they'd killed her for it.

He crossed the Kidron brook and climbed onto the hill of Olives in the night. King David went the same way, and spent the night praying in Gesthemene in the dark garden.

Maybe one of Jeshua's students, taken in the fight at the temple or at Siloam's pool, sold him to the Romans to save himself. As David was betrayed, so maybe one of those men betrayed him, Simon Peter Bargiona or some other.

"Oh my love," she says, "I would have died for you."

She climbs out of the wheat fields and into the small trees at the top of the hill. Again she imagines a low rustling in the brush. And she imagines the temptation which protects her, a man just out of sight behind a turning of the road. Her bare feet search for the warmth of his footprints. Her cold cheeks feel the warmth of his breath. Perhaps he's not a man but an animal, a bull or a big ram with gilded horns and flowers tied around his neck. Perhaps he is her sacrifice to the spirits of hell. In her mind's eye she can see Jeshua of Nazareth, and he's walking on a road darker than hers. The air is not scented with the smell of juniper and wild grass, but it comes out of the mouths of dead men. The noises around him aren't the chittering of bats, the song of grasshoppers and frogs, the barking of a dog or a fox. But on his road under the earth he is surrounded by the whimpering spirits of dead men. And the voices which reach him from the turning of that road belong to Anubis and Baal and monkey-headed Hermes, who lead him onward and forever into Sheol.

She imagines him nearby. As her road climbs up into the hills, his is climbing down. He is naked save for the winding sheet which Simon the leper's daughters made for him. It flaps around his body in a wind colder than this. No, she can't bear it. On the road in front of her there is a red bull with golden horns and a yellow mane. He will bend his fore-legs and kneel down before the throne of the great God. He will dig his horns into the dust and ask for the heart of Jeshua of Nazareth, who loved her once.

In her mind she takes the beast by its gold horn. It gives its life into her hand. With the point of a spear she cuts its life out of its breast, and the blood of the bull pours down through its thick hair, down onto the ground. She imagines Jeshua pausing on his road in that cold desert where it never rains. The blood of the bull seeps down into the earth and falls around him, purified, and he reaches out his hands. The blood will reach him not as water but as light, will spatter him with light in that dark place. He will wash his face in light, and it will drip from his dark hair and beard, run down his chest.

But who betrayed him to his death? She is faithful and will always be. If she becomes a whore on the streets of Jerusalem, still she will be faithful. Every sabbath night she will make this journey. She will fill her basket with herbs and make this journey till she's an old woman.

* * *

That night Jeshua's mother comes to the village of Bethany, west of the city, close by the hill of Olives. The men grunt and struggle with their wheelbarrow in the narrow, pitted street. Miles away, Mary of Magdala travels a highway that is broad and plain toward Joppa and the coast. She comes out through a stand of oaks, and then the road curves down. The sky is pink over the eastern hills.

Now she finds herself among the tombs close by the village of Aceldama. White limestone breaks in ridges from the ground, and among them rich men from the city have made gardens. Walls of heaped stones line the road on either side.

Standing in darkness under the trees, she can see flickering shadows in the gardens, where people have set down lamps against the inside of the walls. Farther back, they've set lamps against the cliff faces. Some tombs are dark, but many are lit.

Mary listens for the sound of voices but hears nothing. She didn't know the place was so big, a city of tombs. She comes down the hill where the road narrows and slips through a small cleft. And her heart sinks when she sees hundreds of lights filling the bowl of a valley on the other side. The lights spread out into the hills.

She didn't guess her husband's tomb would be hard to find. Where are all the others? The old woman paid her cousin Joseph thirty silver pieces for an alcove in his new tomb. Yet which is it of all these? She expected just a few lamps to guide her, and the voices of the people. Surely they didn't precede her by so much. They were carrying her husband's body from Golgotha.

And if she's wrong, if they've had the time to come and go, why didn't she meet them on the road? Surely this is the right place. In a moment she is caught by doubts. She stops and bows her head, resting her hand on the stone wall beside her. She hasn't eaten in a long time.

Then she begins to wander among the gardens. She walks along the face of the cliff, along a line of seven round stones which seal the entrances to seven caves. But they have pyramids of small stones laid against them, and she imagines she can tell they haven't been disturbed. Near one of them a wick burns in a clay pot of oil, punctured with a row of holes along its rim. She picks it up and holds it in her palm. The clay is warm, and she can feel the shifting of the oil.

A crowd of women must have come out before dusk to light these lamps. Mary raises the clay pot, and by its light she sees for the first time the flowering laurels against the bank, the bird's eye lilies and the red anemones under the carob tree. At the same time, as if freed by the sight of them, the smell of the dew and the wet flowers comes to her on the dawn breeze. It is a cold year. These flowers are late.

But now already as the sky grows pink she feels the presage of a warm day. She puts down her empty basket and her lamp. Then she strips her red shawl from her shoulders and hangs it over the low wall. She won't need it. Today is the sabbath, and this place is too far from Jerusalem. No one will come here today, and she will share it with the insects and the birds, the flowers and the spirits of the dead. She pulls up her sleeves and then pulls her dress open to examine her ribs where she has cut herself. The long sore wound is filled now with sticky scabs.

She rips a piece of linen from her clothes. She finds a lamp that has gone out, yet still has oil in it. Sitting on some fallen rocks, she pours oil over the cloth and presses it into her side as Jeshua taught her, while at the same time humming a little song. It comes out of nowhere, nonsense words, pieces of tunes. She sits humming and singing as the sun comes up, and when it breaks over the eastern hills she steps into the road and makes a little dance, some steps that she remembers learning in her father's house in Magdala. A slave taught her, a girl younger than herself.

She spins round and round until she falls against the rocks, out of breath. A cloud of flies hovers around her, and she listens to the buzzing of the flies.

Then she must have fallen asleep in the new grass, because when she wakes up, the sun is high in the eastern sky. She has a row of mosquito bites along her forearm, and her face is hot and swollen.

There's no wind. The air seems thick and hard to breathe. The sky is cloudless, yet not blue, but white.

She rolls onto her back and presses the tips of her fingers against her cheeks. She sits up and tries to rise, except a sudden blackness overtakes her, and she has to crouch down until it passes. How thirsty she is! In time she lifts her head, climbs up to her knees.

Some heaviness in the air has gathered the horizons in, and she saw farther at dawn than now at mid-day. It is as if a cloud surrounds her, and she wonders if it's everywhere or only here in the city of the dead. Then she remembers what she saw on the white hill of Golgotha, the horse or donkey kicking over the lamp, and she imagines Jerusalem on fire, the smoke rising from the earth, and she is standing in a fog of smoke which hurts her eyes. This day Jeshua is in hell, and perhaps smoke is escaping from the hole he made. Perhaps he burrowed down into the underworld and lit a fire there. She has an image of him standing with the burning brand, stooping under the low roof of slanted rock, black and hot from the flame. With the brand he's holding Cerberus at bay, while around him press the ghosts of the old men. There in that place it's as if he were the only one alive, the only one with youth and strength and color in his face, while around him drift Micah, Amos, Daniel, Ezekiel, and a hundred others, their pale faces bruised where he has slapped them and pulled out their beards. The world is burning from the inside out, and he has lit the fire.

It is not until hours later that she finds the tomb. It stands away from the road, cut into a bank of tumbled stone. A boulder seals the entrance to the cave.

It is the garden of Joseph the camel driver. There are laurel bushes with white flowers among the rocks. Nor has the grass withered, but it grows around the base of a small almond tree. Massed between the white boulders are hyssop plants and dandelions.

But already when she comes there, her basket is full of flowers. She has taken bitter grass from the stone walls, and hyacinth and crimson lilies, which she brings in her basket to the mouth of the tomb.

Joseph of Arimathea's name is carved onto a rock beneath the almond tree. She looks for the new footprints that have bent the grass and marked the earth. She finds nothing, but imagines: Here's where they laid him while they rolled the stone back in its slot. Here's where the dirt is broken, here's where the stone is chipped. Here's where they stood, Miriam and Salome and Simon the leper's daughter.

They didn't take the time to seal the boulder with loose stones. They built no cairn against the rock. It was too dark for them to see what she now sees, a hole at the bottom of the boulder where it fits into the cave's mouth. Lying on her side, Mary thrusts her arm up to her shoulder into the tomb itself. Surely where her arm goes, rats and snakes can also pass.

She can't roll the stone away. Two men couldn't do it. She lies on her side and rests her head against the earth. Moment by moment she expects tears will come, but they do not.

She rolls onto her back. The sun is hot. Here's where the women stood, crying and lamenting as the men pushed the boulder into place. What songs had they sung? Had they told the last story of Jeshua of Nazareth, the story of his death? She knows why they wanted to keep her away. She could sing a song they didn't know, that no woman but herself could sing. Certainly not an unmarried child from Bethany. Certainly not a fisherman's wife. Certainly not a laundry woman from the hills of Galilee, who buried three husbands and now buries her son.

Mary of Magdala rises to her knees. She presses her face into the hole. She breathes in the black air, hoping to catch a smell of some perfume, some rottenness, something other than the earth and the damp stone. She stays there for some minutes, then reaches behind her for her basket. She takes handfuls of flowers and thrusts each one into the hole in the rock, as far as she can reach with her whole arm.

Now she imagines the inside of the tomb. The stone is rolled back to show the dark night. The cave is lit with lamps. Among those women, not even Jeshua's mother has more right to be there than his wife, more right to lay him out on the stone slab and close his eyes, and wash his body with cold water and oil. In her mind she rubs cold oil into his wounds, sealing them up. In her mind she washes the dust out of his hair and combs it clean. She kisses his hands and feet. She lays her head upon his chest for the last time, while the women turn away. The men have not come in, but they stand guard outside the door.

They have brought a hundredweight of flowers, as if for a king. Salome of Capernaum spreads them in the alcove where he'll lie. The others hold the winding cloth. They have no tears, but she is weeping as she rubs his chest and neck with perfume, a double handful of thick oil. They hide their eyes as she rubs the oil along his legs, into his hair, not forgetting his man's part which only she has the right to touch.

With eyes averted, they hold out the roll of cloth. Their eyes are dry as stones. They try to find the words of a lament with their rough voices, but then quickly they are silent, shamed by her tears. And by the beauty of her voice, because she's singing now as she wraps her husband in his cloth. They don't like this song. They don't understand it. Later they will make her suffer for it. But she does what she wants. A bundle of myrrh is my love to me, and he will lie all night between my breasts—a slave's song, a whore's song. But once in Tiberias she sang this song to him, and he had smiled.

Outside in the hot afternoon, she puts the last of her flowers in through the hole in the rock. Then she seals up the hole with dirt and pieces of small stone. She writes with a stick in the dry dirt in front of the tomb: This is the King of the Jews.

She goes to wait under the almond tree. She touches the wound over her ribs. Hungry, thirsty, she tries to eat some grass but spits it out.

Then after an hour or so, she goes back to the stone. With her bare foot she wipes away what's written in the dirt. She pulls away the stones she'd packed into the hole, and lies down again, and puts her hand into the hole again. She can feel a coldness on her fingers, a current of air inside the tomb. Outside where she is, the day is hot and still.

Evening comes. The lamps have burnt invisible all day, but now she sees them.

When she falls asleep under the almond tree, this is what she dreams: she is standing on a high rock over the desert in the shelter of some trees. Below her she sees the battle formations, drawn up in the sunlight in the desert grass. The sun shines on their helmets.

The soldiers' shields are like mirrors of bronze. The spikes of their spears, which rise above their heads, are like the golden tassels of a wheat field.

Now there's a wind out of the desert, and the clouds hide the sun. Now it is dark, and the wind blows through the soldiers. From the rock she can see the wind blow through the spears, tossing them aside in swirling patterns, a storm among the wheat. The horses rear on their hind legs, and many fall.

Who will stand against God's anger? Who will stand against that wind? Now there's lightning among the clouds, and an army of beasts comes out of the desert. Each beast has the face of a man or a woman, according to its kind. There are leopards and bears, lions and wild wolves. No soldier can resist them and their leader, who stands on a chariot drawn by bulls. He has a javelin in each hand, which is the lightning. His hands and feet are marked and bleeding. His face is hidden by the storm.

* * *

Very early in the morning on the first day of the week, she is waked by the sound of horses. They are stamping on the road, and she hears the jingle of their bridles. She hears the voices of the men.

The sky is gray and soft. The grass is wet. She lies wrapped in her shawl under the almond tree. After a moment she rolls onto her back, touches her swollen eyes.

She listens to the stamp of horses on the road, the sound of voices. She knows the soldiers are coming to the tomb. For a moment she wonders whether she should let them come and find her. Or she wonders whether she has the strength to move. Her side hurts. Her stomach hurts, and she is thirsty.

But finally she's afraid. Fear lets her move. She gets to her hands and knees, and then climbs into a gully between the rocks. There she half sits, half lies down as best she can. She leans against the rough stone and listens to the beating of her heart.

She hears the voices of the men, grunting and cursing in the language of the snowy woods. She hears the grinding of the stone. She hears the sound of it falling as they roll it over on the grass.

Joseph the camel driver sold his tomb to the old woman. Now Mary thinks he must have sold the news of what he did.

More curses and talking, and the sound of horses. Joseph is a rich man, she knows. He loves nothing but money and the Romans who protect it. But who was the traitor who brought the soldiers to Gesthemene?

She peers over the boulder. There are three horses by the almond tree, eating mint in Joseph's garden. A man stands with them. The stone is down, and she is almost glad, because she thinks she'll see Jeshua again now after all. The door is open. And if she stands up now and climbs down to the garden, maybe they won't prevent her from seeing him, touching him, touching his hair, closing his eyes. Maybe she's done nothing wrong, nothing unforgivable. Yet she's too weak to stand.

Two soldiers climb out of the tomb. They have to stoop. The sun is rising, and when they stand up it is shining on their helmets. Her eyes are dazzled, and she looks away. But not before she recognizes the older of the two soldiers on the hill, the one with the yellow beard and the white scar, who touched her underneath the cross. Now he stands on the right side of the open tomb. The man on the left side is a stranger.

They're leading the horses to the road. Then they're gone before she calls out, before she realizes they've taken nothing. Instead they came through like God's whirlwind, blew through suddenly and then went, touching nothing, leaving the stone down.

Once more she imagines they are creatures from another world. Now they're gone and the noise is gone, and the cloud of dust has settled on the road. She tries to stand, but can't. But the sun warms her now, and she sits for a long time, gathering strength. Sitting, she remembers the young soldier who touched her on her cheeks and eyes at Golgotha. She imagines they must have killed him. The older ones must have blamed him and told lies, for he was innocent. Did they beat him, or hit him with a sword, or crucify him on the empty cross?

Now she climbs down through the rocks on her hands and knees. At the same time she is praying. You took me from my mother's womb. You made me hope when I was on my mother's breasts.

Later she prays from the same song: Dogs come around me, wicked men. I count my bones while they look and stare. They divide my clothes.

She crawls into the garden past the stone. The soldiers and horses left no footprints, no marks, except the stone is down. Three men couldn't budge it, it's so big. She uses it to climb up to her feet. The sun has risen, and the day is hot. There are shadows all around her. Birds come.

Her hands are trembling as she crosses the wet grass and stands in the cave's mouth. She no longer expects to see her husband's body, so she's not surprised. She climbs into the empty alcove and lies there shivering in the dark until Jeshua's mother comes for her later that same day.

CHAPTER TWO:
MARY OF BETHANY, CLEOPAS'S WIFE

These are the days the old men foretold. The life of the world is divided into twelve parts. Ten parts are gone already and half of the eleventh part. Now three animals have come out of the whirlwind. The first is a bear with eagle's wings and the heart of a man. The second is a lion and three ribs are in his mouth. The third is a leopard with nine heads along his back.

There is no doubt. Three captains hold our city against the Romans. The lion is Simon Gioras, and the bear is Eleazer the zealot. The leopard is that devil, John of Gischala, and the nine heads are his nine sons. These men have fought each other in the streets of Jerusalem. They have filled their stomachs with the flesh of their own people. Because of their sins, the four winds have blown down the walls of the city and the temple is destroyed.

The winds are the legions of Vespasian Caesar, the fifth, the tenth, the fifteenth, and the twelfth. The tenth is camped on the hill of Olives. I have seen the soldiers breaking down the doors of the empty houses, looking for food. Lepidus Sulpicianus, Caesar's captain, came into our garden and told me I wouldn't be disturbed. "Old woman," he called me in the Greek language. I gave him water. The countryside near here is empty, and the people have run away.

The four winds circle the head of the fourth beast, Caesar's son, who is a giant covered with hair, terrible and strong, with iron teeth. Already this beast has crushed the other three. A fire came from his mouth and burned the fortress and the temple. Soot blows on my roof.

Jerusalem is burning. The cities of the world are burning. A man comes to the house, an old man, and in him I recognize the one they called Bartholomew when he was with the rabbi in the old days. He is hungry. Sometimes he sees me, sometimes not. He has come from the fighting, and he brings me news of the end of the world. Four Caesars murdered during a single year, and Rome a heap of ashes, and thousands of men and women, Jews and gentiles, killed in the rabbi's name. Eaten by wild beasts in the arena. Simon Peter Bargiona and Saul of Tarsus are dead, one crucified, one killed with a sword. When I hear this my heart rises and for a moment I'm glad, especially when I think of the sharp sword.

Bartholomew escaped out of Jerusalem when the walls were thrown down. He is walking toward Pella, in Perea among the gentiles. A few of the synagogue, the rabbi's students and their followers among the Jews, have gone in the past years. But the road is dangerous and no message was sent. Most stay with the zealots in the city and die with them.

I light the lamp and put it on the table for comfort's sake. I put a fire on the hearth. There's no wood, so I break up the chair which belonged to my father. Tonight the darkness will not come. Fire burns behind the hill. Bartholomew the Canaanite is lying down against the wall on the straw mat. I kneel over him with water from the cistern in a cup. He can't stop talking, though the words are hurting him. I have barley flour which we were keeping for my brother's supper. In ten days there will be no more. God will provide, or won't.

I mix the flour and water while I listen to the old man. His beard is yellow, his face has sunk into the bones of his skull. He has wounds on his chest and belly, which he tries to hide from me. There's no blood in him. The cuts, though recent, are already dry. His voice is dry. "From where we watched the mountain boiled with fire from top to bottom. Caesar's son lit the fire in the sanctuary and the soldiers set their torches to the roofs. Simon the zealot and Matthew were cut down before the altar stone."

"Shut your mouth." The words are in my mind but I say nothing. My heart rises when I think of Simon and Matthew, cowards who betrayed my lord. But on the night the Romans took him, they ran. That was years ago when I was a young girl, but I can't forgive them. Kneeling over the old man to give him the food, I can't forgive him either. I have made a soup of hot water, barley meal, and salt. I try to stop his mouth with it. In a moment he is silent with his own thoughts, and I can move about the house. When I come back I see he is asleep, curled on his side. There is a smell. When I move him, I see he has soiled his legs with blood and dirty water. And something more. In his bowels were thirteen gold coins from the Jewish mint. One coin for each man at the table that night. One for each man who betrayed Jeshua of Nazareth, and then one left over.

Bartholomew ate the coins before he left the city. I'm surprised he walked this far. He recognized the house. He was often here in the old days. I remember his black curls and nervous face, the way he picked his lips. Now I make him comfortable, though I am angry because of the dirt. I sweep the coins over the stones. They are stamped from the first year of the rebellion, when the zealots ambushed the twelfth legion and drove them from the city. Simon Gioras promised the Romans their lives if they gave up their weapons. Then he murdered them when they were helpless, though it was the sabbath. Now he's punished. All Jerusalem is punished. This is the fourth year since that time.

I don't touch the coins. They roll and clatter and make a wet mark on the stones. Gold has no use here at the end. There is nothing to buy, no one to sell it. I sweep the coins over the threshold and stand watching the fire behind the hill.

Then I turn back into the inner room where my brother lies on his bed. He's also an old man, withered to bones, scarcely bigger than a child, scarcely alive now after all these years. But the rabbi raised him, and maybe he'll live forever.

I light the lamp above him and stand watching his lips, his grizzled chin, listening to his slow, tiny breath. A fly crawls on his cheek. He never wakes now, never opens his eyes.

Then I turn back to clean the floor and wash the stones as is my custom, dawn and dusk. I sweep the hearth and wipe the benches in the big room, taking pleasure in the work. It leads me to remember the girl I once was, when I never touched a broom, and my father beat me for refusing. It leads me to remember others who have passed though these rooms, Sarah the Egyptian, and Sapphira of Jericho, and the rabbi's mother. My eyes are dry but I can hear a small sound in my throat. Before I finish sweeping, I throw down the broom.

Now my sister is there, standing on the threshold, a smile in her toothless mouth. She carries a bundle of juniper sticks on her shoulder, and she holds a dead pigeon in her right hand. Where has she found these treasures? She drops them inside the door, then bends over the sleeping body of Bartholomew the Canaanite. With trembling hands, I bring the bird onto the hearth and start to pluck away the feathers. I hear my sister muttering behind me, and I know what she's doing. I hear her pry the brick out of the floor, and into that empty hole she drops the coins that I had swept into the dust. "I found it caught in a bush with a broken wing," she says. "Now look."

I tell her about Bartholomew, though she doesn't ask. But she has searched him and brought away a bag of leather scraps which he was hiding in his waist. I think she didn't recognize his face. Her memory is bad. "Let me," she says now, as she washes her hands. She takes the bird away, then sits down with it in her lap and pulls away its soft feathers. "Read," she says, nodding toward the table where she has left the bag. Then I go into the circle of the lamp and sit there reading, as Sarah taught me. Those leather scraps are covered with small words in the Greek language, and after a moment I sit down on the stool. I stumble over the phrases, but I am reading stories of the rabbi's life, and Martha listens as she plucks and draws the bird, and sets it over the fire.

My mouth is full of water from the smell of cooking and the burning juniper. Still I continue, and I read the story of how the rabbi healed a madman. On another scrap, I see him curse a fig tree and it withers up. Or I read how he once told the men to pay their taxes to Tiberius Caesar. The words taste rotten on my tongue. I read how Judas Iscariot sold the rabbi to the priests for thirty silver pieces, though Pontius Pilate tried to save him. Then he was crucified between two men at Golgotha, and Simon of Cyrene carried his cross.

These are all lies. I read how five girls waited for their bridegrooms. Martha says, "Sister, how lucky we have lived so long and known such men."

She has brought a cup of wine from inside the house. Where did she find it? She puts it out for me, then brings the pigeon on a wooden plate. All this time I have been reading her the story of the rich man, Ananias, how he sold a piece of land in Jericho and offered up the money to Simon Peter. How he lied about the money, and God struck him and Sapphira dead out of his hand.

Martha says, "Come sister, eat."

But there is a shaking in my stomach. "Is this how it was?" I say. "Do you remember?"

Martha sits on her stool, picking at the bones with greasy fingers. I read to her how Pontius Pilate let the rabbi's mother take his body down to Joseph's tomb in Aceldama, far from here. My sister nods and smiles. When I look up again, I see she's falling asleep. She has walked a long way looking for food. Now her cheek is on the table, and I reach and lay my fingers on her forehead. She suffers me to touch her, and her eyes close.

Now everyone is sleeping in my house. I put the book aside, get to my feet. Standing on the threshold, I look into the yard. I step out under the sycamore tree, where the lower branch was broken by the rope, the weight of the falling body. The drought weakened the tree and the place has never healed, the split branch.

After Sarah left, my sister threw a rope over that branch. She showed me the place under the bricks, and gave me Sarah's ring to sell. I was going to Jerusalem to see the head and body of Thaddeus the zealot—this was when they were displayed at the Antonia. This was after he attacked the legion on the hill of Olives—he was a bold man, and I wanted to go see him. But my strength failed. I went with Jonathan the hired man, and we came back before we were expected, and we came in through the gate, and there was my sister Martha caught like a rabbit in a snare. She was wearing her bleached woolen dress as if she were a bride. The rope was around her neck, and we had to cut it loose. The breaking branch had saved her. But she doesn't remember even this.

I untie my hair, my long black hair streaked now with gray. I shake it out over my shoulders, and in the red light of the evening I go down to the bottom of the garden and stand before the seal of the tomb. Then I light the lamp, and with the lamp in my hand I find the hidden entrance to the chamber under the stone bank. On my hands and knees I crawl in through the hole.

It's the tomb cut for my father and my brother Lazarus, who never used it except for a few days. But the rabbi is here. Inside, the walls are dry. Here is the stone box with its heavy lid. The alcoves are all empty. There's a dusty smell and also a small fragrance, because I used to come here and burn incense when I had money. The ceiling is too low to stand upright. Instead I sit in a place that has been worn smooth by sitting, and put the lamp down in the sand. Over it the stone is charred, discolored.

"Jeshua, arise," I murmur. Once I sat by his knees and heard him say how he would burn the temple and rebuild it in three days. Now Mount Moriah is in flames. The stone of sacrifice is broken. The floor of the sanctuary has been defiled. The box is broken and the treasure scattered, as he predicted, as he tried to do. All this has happened on the tenth day of the month of Ab, or Lous in the Greek calendar.

With my own ears I heard him say when Jerusalem is ringed with armies and its walls are thrown down, it will be a token of the day of vengeance and the night that has no morning. Many have seen beasts of heaven and soldiers fighting in the clouds. "Some of you will not know death," he said, "before these things will come." I was the youngest of that gathering. Now Simon and Matthew are dead these last few days, and Bartholomew is dying, and if there are others left alive, I have not heard.

Who was this man who robbed me and my sister? Who took away our father, brother, husbands, children and then put us alone into the world, though we were ordinary women? Now as I sit here, I let my weariness possess me so I can almost see against the wall between the tombs a chair set in the shadows for the ancient of days, and the hair of his head is like white wool. He shows me a vision which I strain to see in the black darkness beyond the circle of the lamp, the house of Israel flattened by the whirlwind and the beams and ornaments cast down. With all my heart I strain to see how in its place the son of man will build a new house higher and stronger. Its gates are made of gold. A thousand thousand, and ten thousand times ten thousand stand before him. All the dead stand there, and the books are opened, and the judgment made. From every land the people will bring incense to the house of the great God, and there will be no other house for them to live in. The mountains and the sea will be made calm. Wolves and lambs will eat grass on the hillside, and the leopards, bears, and lions will eat straw. Serpents will sleep between the children and will not harm them, for God's hand will be on their heads.

* * *

His image is before me now, and it comes out of the rough darkness. His big arms and shoulders. His big chest and thighs. When I was a child he visited my father's house. In the evening he picked me up and put me on his knee, and I remember the hardness of his hand when I grabbed hold of his thumb, the hill of muscle in his hand, the heaviness of his arm. I thought his flesh was different from my flesh. The hair grew thick on his wrists and the backs of his hands. It grew under his shirt and up his neck to mix into his beard. I sat staring at his face, his big nose. His thick lips and broken teeth, evidence of some fight or beating.

There was no beauty in him, nothing to attract a woman, as the prophet warned us. He sat by the fire in my father's chair while I sat on his knee. His clothes smelled of smoke. His hair shone with oil.

Sometimes when one of the others was talking he would whisper in my ear—"Don't listen to that one. He's a fool."

He spoke less than any of them, though he was their teacher. The rebels talked the most, Judas Sicarius, Simon Peter Bargiona, Simon the zealot, and the sons of thunder. These men had fought against the Romans with Menachem of Galilee and others, as the rabbi also had, years before. They had fought against Pilate's soldiers with Barabbas and the sicarii, but over time the zealot captains had rejected them, chased them away. Now they roamed through Galilee, Judaea, and across the Jordan, shunned and threatened by both sides in that war.

Simon Bargiona was talking. He stood with his legs splayed out, hands on his stomach, sweat on his bald head. Later after the rabbi's death, he became fat from of all the money he took. But even in those days he was fatter than the rest. That, with his smallness, had made him ask to be called "Peter," which means rock. He made up a story about how Jeshua named him as a sign of favor. But I never heard the rabbi call him anything but "Simon," or else "Bargiona" when he wanted to make fun of him—meaning "outcast." Barabbas himself had given him that name to punish him for cowardice.

"Don't listen to him," the rabbi whispered in my ear. "Watch him puff out his belly. He's always talking about fighting."

But I was watching my father, his sad face. I could tell he thought I was too old to sit on the rabbi's knees. I could tell he thought I should be helping my sister as she made the food, so to hurt him I leaned back. Now I saw him close his eyes, saw his lips move, and at the same time my sister came in with a plate of beans and oil. "Come," she said to me. My father opened his eyes. Bargiona rubbed his hands together at the sight of food—"She's right. Go to your sister. You're not a child any more."

It made me angry, the way he told me what to do in my father's house. I leaned back against the rabbi's chest. But then I felt his hands push me away, and I stood on the floor beside him. He asked, "What are you saying?"

But then my sister Martha—"Rabbi, don't you care she has left me to serve you by myself? She's been with you all this time."

Then I was eager to join her, because I thought my father might hit me when the guests were gone, because of his embarrassment. He made a motion with his foot. I stepped forward, but I felt the rabbi's hand on my shoulder. "Martha," he said. "We don't need much. Mary has helped us just by sitting here. Nevertheless," he went on after a pause, and I could tell he was looking at my father. "Go to your sister," he told me.

He had a face that moved and changed expression even when he sat without speaking. A child could read his thoughts. He made you want to please him, that was all. Those who sat with him watched his face to learn what they should feel: gladness from his gladness, scorn from his scorn. What makes greatness in a man? It comes suddenly, a sign from God. It does not appear in children.

Still, he was not as ugly as my father Simon, called "the leper" because of his big head and hairless, lion-like face.

Already I had felt a heat from men as I was growing. I had felt their stares. Sometimes I thought my sister was the lucky one, because she took after my father. But what I'm saying is from the rabbi I never felt a warmth of that kind. People talk now of the love that used to flow from him, but I never felt anything like that. He would look at you as if you were a stone or a block of wood. No, the love was what came out of other people.

The love and the crimes also. Maybe all of us who knew him, even the thieves and liars, can find a way to blame themselves for his death. This is my way: The words he spoke that night changed me. Not once before and not once since has any man told me that it is better to keep still than serve him. I wanted to know things so my words could bring a smile to his face or else a frown. As I said, his way of teaching was to be silent.

This was something I told no one, because it couldn't be told. In our country women work under their husbands so they can raise up sons in Israel. The rabbi said, "Unhappy is the pregnant woman with her breasts full of milk." Is it any wonder I turned away from my father at that moment? Simon the leper was a rich man with a stone house and many animals. There was no reason for me to get up before the others to fetch water, light the fire. In other families they spoke Greek, and slaves taught the daughters how to read. In every town you could see the Greeks and Romans and the Jews who learned from them. Among the gentiles, I thought, women are free. Cleopatra had reigned in Egypt. Alexander's mother had been a great queen.

So this is how I blame myself. It was my vanity that led to my brother's death, and through him to the rabbi's death on the day of preparation for the feast, in the sixteenth year of the reign of the Emperor Tiberius, when I was twelve years old. There were soldiers from the Antonia garrison camped in a field outside our village of Bethany, west of Jerusalem. Roman slaves were working on the Jericho road. Chained together in long lines, they squatted in the red dust, hammering stones into gravel. They were prisoners from a war in the east.

The soldiers sat in the shade of the locust trees. They wore leather armor and at mid-day when the sun was hot, they stripped off their leather caps. They had no beards. Their hair was clipped short. Women I had never seen brought water so that they could wash their sweating, sunburned faces. I saw this from far away behind a bush. Several days went by. I came to watch them eat their lunch.

I'd seen Roman soldiers before, of course, when I was a child and on feast days we would go into the city. But these were different from the ones I'd seen. Some held long spears. Others played with dice under the trees. One spoke to me when I was standing before daybreak at the well. I went in the morning and he came out of the cold fog before I turned away. I had the big jar on my head. He laughed and spoke to me in Greek.

His name was Cleopas. He was from Sidon on the coast.

But I wasn't the only woman to come to the well so early. Someone must have seen us, though I wore my shawl over my face. I was only there for a few moments. Later my father closed me up inside the store room by the barn. I kicked a hole in one of the bags of barley so it ran out on the ground.

My mother died when I was young. I knew nothing of the world between men and women. But I knew how to disobey, which every servant knows. Cleopas had told me where to meet him. I crept out before dawn and walked under the trees.

Now I wonder if my brother guessed where I was going, why he didn't call to me. I knew enough to be ashamed. But maybe he thought he could fight a soldier and be safe. What Cleopas was doing was a crime, because of our Jewish law.

My brother was twenty-one years old. He had a knife with a hooked blade. When Cleopas pulled aside the cloth and put his hand on my face beside the dry well after no more than a few words of strange talk, my brother Lazarus came off the hill. Cleopas shouted for his friends, and then I ran away. I ran home and crawled into my corner of the store room among the sacks of grain. Later Martha came to see what was the matter. Our neighbor's sons brought Lazarus and laid him in his bed. He wasn't bleeding, but his body was swollen and bruised. Covered with his cloak, he lay as if asleep. When he stopped breathing and his heart stopped, they put him in the tomb.

My father sent a message to Jeshua of Nazareth, where he was staying in Perea across the Jordan river. In two days he came, for Lazarus's sake, and he and his students took supper with my father. When the meal was finished, I went in with a jar of ointment I had found in my father's store room, a pound of spikenard in an alabaster box. It was the most valuable thing my father had there, an ointment he was keeping for his burial. I think I was angry he hadn't used it on my brother's body. When the meal was over I came with the box in my hands, thinking I could waste it while my father sat by and said nothing. But when I saw the rabbi's face I started to cry. I knelt at his feet and my tears came out of me. I put my forehead in the space between his feet. He never moved.

His feet were big and hard and calloused and the skin was cut and broken from walking on the world's roads. The nail of his big toe was cracked. Blood and dust had entered in. I held his feet in my hands, crying over his bruises, and forgot my anger. I broke open the alabaster box and washed his feet with the ointment, to soothe his skin and soothe the ragged cuts.

The ointment's bitter smell rose out of my hands. It stung my eyes, but I didn't look up. I heard Simon Bargiona's voice, which was beautiful and low. I heard him say, "Master, how can you let this woman touch you? Don't you know how she was taken by a soldier, a Greek? In the town they are already calling her the wife of Cleopas. Judas Sicarius has gone to the Antonia fortress to complain. He was to have married her."

That was the first I'd heard of that. Judas Sicarius was a shy man with a spotted face. I'd liked him for his bandit's name, when first I'd seen him in the rabbi's company. I had to think he was one of the sicarii—zealot warriors who carried hidden daggers. I used to peer at him and search him with my eyes, wondering where he kept it in his clothes.

I knelt down, and the tears came out of me. Simon Bargiona hadn't guessed I'd gone to meet Cleopas of my own will. For a moment I was happy for the wounds of Lazarus, that he hadn't woken to betray me. The ointment's bitter smell was all around.

Then I heard the rabbi's voice. He spoke to my father—"What do you say?"

And my father—"She has no right to touch you."

Maybe he was angry about the ointment. I thought, they don't know I'm to blame, because of what I did. But even so they blame me because the Greek touched my face, that's all.

The rabbi said, "You think like pharisees." Then to my father—"I came to your house to hear your prayers for Lazarus. You gave me no water for my feet. But this woman has washed my feet with tears and dried them with her hair. I tell you he who has no sins will never be forgiven, because he does not love me like this woman."

And then to Simon Peter—"There was a usurer who had two debtors. One owed five hundred denarii, and one owed fifty. When they couldn't pay, the usurer forgave them both. Tell me which debtor loved him more."

I was thinking about Judas Sicarius. As the rabbi was speaking, I began to cry again. He was not one like these others, who would have called me a whore even if Cleopas had broken into my father's house to attack me.

But I heard Peter Bargiona's rich, soft voice—"That's what I mean, about the usurer. This ointment could have been sold for five hundred denarii."

I raised my eyes to the rabbi's face and saw him smile—"Let her alone."

After supper he went walking in the garden. Because of what had happened, my father was afraid to punish me. He gave me my old place to sleep beside the washing room. I looked out the door, waiting for the darkness. Then I took a lamp down to the kitchen garden where the rabbi was walking by himself among the rows of beans. I said, "I was seduced by Cleopas and went to meet him."

"Hush," he said. "Don't say these things out loud, but to yourself."

"I know if you were here, Lazarus would not have died."

He smiled. "God has forgiven you. God will raise your brother on the day."

I started to cry again. "I've heard what people call you. They call you the Christ who will be king."

I held the lamp up to his face. At that moment he was like the Christ to me, his long curls, his beard, his broken face. His eyes were very large, very black in the darkness, and as always he looked at me.

"Mary," he said. "If there is a king in Israel, then he will come out of the house of David as the prophet told us. And the city of David is named Bethlehem. But I'm not from that house, nor have I been to that place. I'm a poor man from Galilee. Now what else?"

But I saw my sister Martha coming down into the garden to search for me. She reached out her hands toward the rabbi and said, "I know God will give you what you ask, because you are the Christ."

But he was smiling as he answered—"There is no one in Jerusalem so stupid someone doesn't call him king of Israel. People call me Christ to throw me from their hearts. But you and your sister, listen to me. Because I cannot raise the dead, don't think I'm a fool."

Other men were in the garden and they came down to interrupt us. They thought that every time the rabbi spoke to us, he shamed himself. Later they abandoned him and only the women were left.

Simon Bargiona was in the bean field with us, and Thomas Didymus, and Philip, and Bartholomew, and many others. They came down through the paths. Jeshua said, "Let me show you." He said, "Where have you laid him?" though of course he knew. We brought him to the tomb at the bottom of the garden. He stood before the seal and shouted, "Lazarus, come out!"

I laughed, because I thought I understood the joke. I said, "Lord, don't raise him up because he stinks. He's been dead for many days."

It was my sin that made me laugh. Jeshua looked at me and I saw his face was sad. When he saw my father limping toward us on his crutch, he turned away. "Enough," he said.

No. But we heard a voice cry out of the grave, and when the men rolled the seal away, my brother sat there with the bandage cloths hanging from his wrists.

Later I wondered if the rabbi raised my brother up from death, why he didn't heal him, too. But that night when Lazarus sat in the entrance to the tomb with the lamps at his feet and the tears flowing from his eyes, none of us could speak. After we took Lazarus indoors, Jeshua of Nazareth would not come in. He stayed in the garden the whole night.

He said nothing to us, but went by himself into the desert to a town called Ephraim. When he came back he was changed. His voice was hoarse with talking. I heard Simon tell my father how for ten days the rabbi hadn't slept except for a few hours at dawn.

Simon Bargiona sat with my father, and they spoke as if I couldn't hear. But I gave them no reason to think I was listening. Since my brother's illness, I hadn't left the house. I hid when the men came to stare at Lazarus. Out of my guilt I fed him with a spoon and washed his clothes and sponged his legs. I swaddled him with strips of linen cloth around his legs and waist, and rubbed his legs with salt and washed the strips out many times a day.

My brother had been a strong man with a face burned red from working in the fields. Now I led him to his straw bed in the inner room and put him down on the white cloth. He made a noise. At first he was calm, but suddenly he struggled up and struck me with his wrists. His water came out of the swaddling strips in a hot stream, soaking the white cloth and the straw. It ran over my hands as I reached toward him.

Once he had taught me letters. Once he had played with me and carried me on his back, three years ago when I was nine years old, before I was a woman.

My sister Martha heard me crying and she came to help. She came behind my brother and put her arms around him. But he twisted away from her on the wet bed. He was shouting and bellowing. He wouldn't be still. Again he hit me, and I fell back with a bruise above my eye. He rolled from the bed and crawled across the floor on his hands and knees, his wet clothes unwinding and dragging across the dirt. He was crawling toward the curtain that kept his room from the big room, and I knew there were men on the other side. I knew they could hear him crying. Maybe they were made helpless by the terrible, formless words which none of us had ever heard before, the language of the tomb. Or maybe they thought it wasn't right to come and help, even though we were two women and he was a strong man. My sister shouted out and hit him from behind.

Then the curtain did move, and someone stood there in the dim light. A tall woman, gaunt and thin, and as she came forward I could see her gray hair and hollow face. It was the rabbi's mother.

My sister held Lazarus around his chest. He was hitting her with his big hands, but when he saw the old woman all the fighting stopped. She opened her mouth to show her teeth, which were clean and white. Her strength came out of her hungry face—my brother stopped his crying. He let Martha take him back to the straw bed, where he sat down and yawned.

The old woman had come to Jerusalem for the passover, which was in a few days. She lived near Sepphoris in Galilee—three days to the northeast. There she'd laid three husbands in their tombs. She washed clothes by the river. She had five sons and one daughter. Later after she died, I heard some people say they found in her bed a statue of Astarte, the Syrian devil, goddess of childbirth. Others praised her, calling her the wife of the one God.

That day in Lazarus's room, I knew nothing of these things. My sister and I stood watching the strength go from our brother into the old woman, and I never thought we were watching something strange or forbidden. Only my sister came and knelt in the half light. She touched her feet and muttered a prayer, which made the old woman laugh.

"What are you saying?" The woman's voice was crude and harsh, and she spoke in the crude language of the Galileans. Her eyes were red, the sockets dark. She had a sweet smell about her which I didn't recognize till I was older. It was beer.

* * *

Now these memories flock around me, and I'm thinking of the days that led to the death of Jeshua of Nazareth, who was betrayed by his own students and condemned. He took their crimes onto himself. If he was guilty, it was only of believing what they said to him. After he raised Lazarus, they gave him no peace. They crowded around him, touching his clothes, kissing his hands. He was sick from sleeplessness. I think when he went to Herod's temple, he believed God would step down from the clouds and meet him there.

Now still it's hard to think about. One night I went to meet him in the garden. I wanted the rabbi's blessing like the others. He stood in the darkness before the empty tomb. I came with a lamp, and I went down on my knees and kissed his hands. "You are the Christ," I murmured, but he interrupted me:

"Will you come with me when we go into the town? You can guide us to the gate. It has been years since I was there."

He was talking about Herod's temple. I was surprised, because I knew how much he hated that place. I said, "My father has forbidden me to go."

He smiled. "All the world will be there."

That was how he dared to speak out in such a place, because he thought the temple soldiers could do nothing in a crowd. He was right.

The world was with him the next morning. People stood outside our house, waiting before dawn, forty at least, women and children as well as men. When the rabbi stepped from the house, barefoot, dressed in his coarse shirt, they stretched out their hands.

Judas Sicarius was there, though he didn't look at me.

The rabbi had sent Simon Bargiona out to find an ass's colt, because of what the prophet said. Whether it was a sign of softness or something else, but he sat down on it, on some colored cloths they'd put down.

I watched his mother spit the bitter juice out of the herbs she chewed. That morning she was angry. I was standing beside her as the people put down palm fronds over the thick dust. I heard her curse, which shocked me.

Martha and my father stayed behind. They'd put Lazarus into a cart so the people could see him. He followed Jeshua in a cart. I stood between the rabbi's mother and someone else, a woman five years older than me.

This was the virgin of Magdala, as men called her to laugh at her. She had the evil eye. But that day she was happy. She grasped me by the hand. Then without asking she remade the cloth over my mouth.

Her hands were always restless, moving. Because she was with the old woman and because they were with Jeshua, I thought they loved each other. But that day as we followed Jeshua in the crowd—the three Marys, stepping on the branches over the dust—the virgin of Magdala held my arm and plucked my sleeve. Her thin fingers hurt my arm. She whispered in my ear. She called the rabbi's mother an old whore. At first I didn't know what she was saying because at the same time she was shouting with the others, "Lord, save us from the tyrants. This is our Jewish king."

That was my glad day. I was free of my father and brother, free of my father's house, and I was following the rabbi to Jerusalem. The trees were in flower. The wind was in our clothes. The road was full of people coming to the city for the feast. I could feel the sun on my head, warming the linen cloth.

We climbed through the terraced fields, full of the young wheat. We came through the orchards of olive trees and the stands of terebinth—all gone now. We climbed the hill, and then before us lay Jerusalem, the narrow valley of the Kidron still in shadow. The walls of Jerusalem, the cliff of Mount Moriah, the long walls of the temple splashed with sunlight, rising above us as we made our descent among the graves, over the stream and up the other side. We came to the Sheep's gate as they blew the trumpets. All around stood the ragged tents of the country people. All around us there were beggars and lepers as we came through the double door, then under the square tower of the Antonia where the Romans kept watch. We climbed the steps onto the mountain. There was a crowd of many hundreds as we came up.

Sometimes the soldiers crucified someone who tried to burn the temple down. But that day the rabbi came in with the crowd, and my heart rose as we climbed up onto Solomon's porch, past the Golden gate, which was always closed. Then we were underneath the cedar roofs of the portico, among the rows of Greek columns, while behind us people carried Lazarus's cage up the high steps. It was the week before the passover, and the court of the gentiles was full of people selling food and clothes. They had put tables inside the Royal porch and the Huldah gates, and where the bridge came from the upper town. I stood on the ramparts looking west over the rooftops, past Herod's towers toward the western hills. The air was clear. The sacrifice had not yet started, and the wind blew from the north.

I stripped my shawl away and let the sun fall on my face. Many of the women on the porch had naked faces, and not just old women like the rabbi's mother. That morning the courts were full of women from the country, where they work uncovered in the fields. Or else from Egypt or Rome. Around me people talked in many languages. I saw Greeks in their short shirts, talking to Philip of Bethsaida and Peter Bargiona's brother. Maybe they wanted the rabbi's blessing, or maybe they sold weapons to the zealots. I saw Philip and Andrew pushing them away. The rabbi's students were trying to make a space for him in the crowd, but it was difficult because there were so many pressing around him, curious for Lazarus's sake. Mary of Magdala was pulling on my arm, talking in my ear, but I couldn't hear her. The noise was too great. Men jostled against us. As always in a place where they can touch us without fear, I could feel their fingers pushing underneath my clothes, for I was held in by the crowd.

In Herod's temple was a court for women. Mary of Magdala spent the day there. The rabbi's mother made a path for us along the inner wall until we found the gate. But this was my glad day, and I didn't mean to spend it in the quiet courts, guarded by Levites and the temple soldiers. I wanted to see what they were selling in the market. I wanted to go through the Royal porch where the men had tables piled with honey rolls and fruit. They had booths where they were selling doves and taking payment for the lambs. Others had boxes of copper bracelets and brass rings, which they laid in rows on strips of cloth.

All these men took payment in bags of grain, or jars of oil or honey, or bunches of herbs, because they were selling to the country people. The money changers also accepted these things, which were piled against the walls near where the animals were kept, or stacked under the tables. These men had lines in front of them. They paid Sidonian silver pennies, which elsewhere were hard to get. Rich strangers who had come to the festival from Alexandria or Damascus also bought these coins, because the priests accepted nothing else for sin offerings and the temple tax.

Men sold caged birds from Africa. They sold copper chains and figs.

The rabbi's mother led me through the crowd. She was from Galilee and wore a patched, coarse dress. Her belt was a rag around her waist. Her bare feet were stained with dust. But she wasn't frightened, and she was taller than many men. In the country, though they live with animals, the women have more strength.

She pushed the people aside and ignored their curses. When someone pushed me down against the stones and called me Cleopas's wife, she raised me up. She expected no money in return. Though I was the daughter of a rich man, like her I wore my only clothes, which my sister had worn before me. I had nothing and she knew it. Unlike many country people, she didn't ask for gifts.

In another part of the court there was a line of lepers sitting in the shadow of the wall. Or they had lost their arms and legs fighting for the Romans—not Jews, of course, but Greeks and Idumaeans. They squinted up at us, but we had nothing to give. Instead we went to stand under the Beautiful gate to watch the jugglers. Near them the rabbi spoke in an empty space where Philip and Andrew had pushed the people back.

He stood in a row of other rabbis talking to their students and the crowds.

Always before I had seen him in my father's house, listening to Simon Bargiona's speeches, or interrupting him and scolding him with small words. Then his voice was sleepy, slow. But now in the court of gentiles I heard it through the noise of the crowd. I could hear him over the other rabbis, who were small, ragged men. His strong arms were raised above his head as he argued with a man who was there, Zacharias, Eleazer's son.

This man was Levite, a servant of the temple. Sometimes I could see his face between the men who were listening, but I couldn't hear him where we stood under the porch, because his voice was low. The rabbi's mother heard him and she told me what he said. It made her smile. She bent down and I smelled her breath. "He asks if a woman marries three times, who will be her husband in God's kingdom?"

I smelled her sweet, perfumed breath. I looked at her strong teeth. She knew Zacharias was talking about her. The Levites don't believe in God's kingdom. But they believe in sons and fathers.

Now others were made bold by the man's question, and they called out questions of their own, which I don't remember. But I remember what the rabbi said. "You say I have no father. But I say call no man father on earth, because we have all one father in heaven. One father who will throw the rich men from their chairs . . . "

Later he closed his eyes and raised his hairy hands. He cursed the priests by name, Annas and his sons, and other men of the sanhedrin. He called them thieves and slaves of Roman tyrants, of Pontius Pilate who had chosen them.

And now the crowd was silent to hear him, because saying these things in Herod's temple wasn't the same as preaching in Galilee. Now his voice rose up into the sky as he cursed the money lenders and the priests—"When Pontius Pilate first came from Rome, he put Caesar's face on a flag and had it carried through Jerusalem. Barabbas and the zealots made him take it down and you supported us. But now Caesar's portrait is in the temple court, ten thousand times ten thousand times, and you say nothing."

He meant the Roman denarii which the shopkeepers were trading in the porch, each one stamped with the head of Tiberius Caesar. "If you carry Caesar's head, then you are Caesar's man. The rest of us will offer God the things that are his own. Every widow who brings a piece of mint to the altar throws in more than all the coins of the rich men."

He meant the poor should not pay taxes, not to Rome nor to the temple. Around him men were quiet. "Worms," he cried, "eunuchs who do nothing. God, my God," he shouted, raising his fists. "I tell you there won't be a wall left standing here."

The rabbi's younger brother Jacob was in the court. Jacob of Alpheus—his father was a Greek. I saw him clearly, saw his eyes, and saw him bend his neck to talk to someone else, a man I did not know up to that time. This man was beautiful in every way. There was a gold color in his hair and on his cheeks. When he smiled, I could see his teeth were good. His name was Thaddeus the zealot, which I learned later.

He smiled, shook his head, then turned aside to spit. But Jacob of Alpheus did not smile. I saw him take the rabbi by the hand, because he'd said too much.

The rabbi's mother brought me with her when she followed them out the gate onto the steps. Lazarus was there. They'd taken him from the cage. Then I should have been suspicious, because I'd seen them carry it up. But my heart was sinking as Jacob gestured for me to come, and I understood why I was there. I was to lead my brother home, now they had no use for him.

It was a hard job to bring him down the steps. I couldn't have done it by myself. He had a rope around his neck, but he stood on the steps and wouldn't move.

Soldiers laughed at me. They were more interested in me than in Jeshua of Nazareth. They were laughing at my brother as he wagged his head. I was afraid until the rabbi's mother came to help. When Lazarus saw her, he stepped down. The rope was easy in my hands.

The rabbi's mother put her shawl around my shoulders. My own mother was dead. But this woman with her ugly face, she kept the men away. As we climbed down through the narrow, crowded, filthy streets to the Sheep's gate, as we walked through the ravine, past the fig trees of Gesthemene and then onto the hill of Olives, I wondered if the rabbi's kindness had come out of her. Maybe because he had no father, and what he learned had not been spoiled by a father's cruelty. A woman has the world against her. We got home after dark, and the house was full of men. The sons of thunder were there, and Judas Sicarius, and all the zealots.

That night I slept with my sister in her bed on the hard floor.

From time to time after the others were asleep, I got up and went to sit outside the curtain of the inner room. I watched the flicker of the light. I listened to the rabbi's voice, too low to understand. But I was happy with the sound of his voice. My father was snoring in his little room, and men were sleeping around the hearth. I think the rabbi talked all night except for a few hours. What Mary of Magdala said or whether she was awake to listen, I don't know. In the morning she got up before dawn and found me outside the curtain, asleep on the floor. She clapped her hands, chased me away, though she was a guest in my father's house.

People told me they had seen a devil in her when the rabbi first found her on the road. He burned herbs and she smelled them, but then the devil came again.

* * *

That day the sun rose behind a shield of clouds. The air was wet. The rabbi's students had all left during the night, except for Philip and Andrew. In the morning they brought him to the cistern and drew water. I stood in the kitchen garden and watched them cut his hair. It fell around his shoulders, and they washed it away. They clipped his beard short like a Roman's.

I suppose they thought he needed a disguise. In the week before the passover, many were arrested every year, because of the riots in the city when Pontius Pilate first came from Rome. Some were let go after the feast was over. Some were crucified at Golgotha on the sixth day of the week.

Often there were small rebellions, but that day the zealots planned for something more. They had spears and knives which they had hidden in Lazarus's cage under the straw, to get them past the guard. After what the rabbi said, they counted on a crowd to hear him speak again. They thought with the crowd's help they could break into the Antonia fortress. The garrison was small, not fifty men. Pilate was not yet inside the city with his regiment.

I believe the rabbi knew nothing of their plans. Unlike him I knew something was wrong. After he was gone into Jerusalem, I helped my sister and brushed the floors, that awful day.

My father chased Mary of Magdala to the courtyard. She wouldn't let us near. Maybe she felt as I did the weight of bad luck. She sat in the shade of the sycamore tree and bit her lips and fingers. She screamed once in the afternoon. I went out to see if I could find some of my master's hair in the dust near the cistern. But when I saw her, I couldn't stand to look at her, and so I ran away.

The roads were full of people from Jericho and across the Jordan. So many people were traveling, they didn't notice a woman by herself. I meant to go into the city. But I was sick to my stomach and my head was light. So in half an hour I stopped at the garden of Gesthemene and sat down under the trees where people camped. I thought if he came back, I would see him on the road.

I sat under the fig trees, staring at nothing. But I heard news among the people, because men spoke as if I weren't there. One man was telling others what he'd heard. Seven Roman soldiers had been ambushed near Siloam's pool. In the temple, on Solomon's porch, the guard had found some weapons in the empty barrels. And a man from Nazareth had broken down the tables of the money changers. He broke the cages of the doves, the lambs, the calves. He chased the dealers down the steps. Priests were carrying water in the court, and he knocked the vessels from their hands.

That spring there were no early figs, because of the cold weather. There were bees among the clover at Gesthemene among the budding leaves. I listened to them and looked at my hands in my lap. As I sat on the ground, my back was straight. I felt a prickling in my shoulders.

Later I saw him coming, led by Thomas Didymus and Thaddeus the zealot. No one recognized the rabbi on the road or in the garden with his hair clipped short. His shirt was ripped. He kept his hand against his cheek, and I thought when he took it away I'd see a bruise.

I'd brought food for him, bread and cheese and a jar of wine from my sister's kitchen. Water and oil for him to wash himself. When I saw him, I uncovered my face. Thomas Didymus saw me, and brought Jeshua to where I sat under the fig tree. "Lord," I said, but more than that I couldn't say. When he sat, I knelt down at his feet. Finally I took courage and looked up again. Thaddeus the zealot was staring at me, and I felt my cheeks grow hot. So I turned my attention to Jeshua of Nazareth. He was looking at the fig tree, which was flowering.

I knelt over his dirty feet. He said nothing to me. He was talking to Thomas Didymus—"There's a tree that brings out leaves and flowers but no fruit."

"You were deceived," murmured Thomas Didymus.

"Because my eyes were closed."

His thoughts moved from place to place. "Did you see them, Thomas?" he continued. "An old man and a boy. God help them, they had laid them on the steps."

I wiped my hands on a napkin. I laid out the food and wine. From time to time I glanced up, and saw Thaddeus the zealot staring at me. He was a beautiful man.

Jeshua of Nazareth took bread without washing, without thanking

God or me. Then he was breaking it between his fingers and throwing crumbs into the dirt until a small bird came down from the tree. Other men were sitting near us in the garden. They stared at him because he broke the law.

"Rabbi," murmured Thaddeus the zealot. "We've a long way to travel before nightfall."

The bird was pecking crumbs out of the dust. Jeshua shook his head. "Is that what you think? That I'll find some cave to hide in in the desert? In Perea? If you spill blood you spill your own."

With the back of my hand I wiped my eyes, smelling the perfumed oil on my fingers. Thomas Didymus said, "You didn't know."

Jeshua shook his head. "For my sake, Thomas. For my sake. When Ben-Judah set a fire in the porch, I knocked the water from their hands. I had the whip in my fist. Is it their sin if they didn't understand? I told them the temple would be broken and then raised up like Lazarus. Now I run when they try to do it. The Romans took Dimas and his brother. They'll be crucified. The soldiers are looking for the rest of them."

"You, too."

"Of course. They were my men."

Thomas Didymus grunted. "They never followed you." He got to his feet. "Enough of this. Let's go."

Maybe Bargiona thought they could have held the city against Pilate and the regiment, when the streets were full of zealots for the passover. Maybe they thought they could hold Caiaphas and the rest of the priests, take them prisoner and no one would defend them, because of the tax money they stole. The people would rise up, as they had under Ezekias, and Judah of Galilee, and Sadok the Levite, and the Lion of Tabor, and Jeshua Barabbas. All they needed was one man to show the way.

Now the rabbi sat looking at the budding fig tree with the wind in its leaves. I said, "My father's house is near by, as you know."

* * *

Mary of Magdala had copper-colored hair, which sometimes she braided and tied up. She sat next to the sycamore tree, staring at the ground, and I could see her dirty, naked legs. Her curls hung down around her shoulders. Her lips were scabbed and bloody, her hands torn from the stones. Her white skin was streaked with dust. Under her black brows, her eyes were fierce with anger, because of the devil, I thought.

She stood up when she saw Jeshua of Nazareth. Her clothes were torn and we could see her naked legs. In the temple the day before, she was ashamed even to show even her face. Now, uncovered, she came toward us over the red dirt of the yard.

Madness gives strength and we all saw it, though we couldn't guess what she would do. Or perhaps the rabbi guessed. She stood in front of him and said nothing except for the small grunts she made as she was hitting him across the cheeks. She struck him on his clipped cheeks, and he stood in front of her with his head bowed so she could reach him. His eyes were closed.

Maybe they all turned against him then, watching him let a woman punish him without resisting. For the sake of Dimas and Gestas, the zealot brothers who were prisoners, for the sake of her torn clothes and dirty hair, they wanted him to strike her down. When he didn't, when he stood with his eyes closed under the sycamore tree, maybe they lost their love for him. Simon Bargiona was there, and Philip, and Andrew. They were standing together at the door of the house, talking to my father.

Thaddeus the zealot went to them, and then the four of them walked away into the twilight without a word to us, pulling their blankets over their faces as they went out the gate. My father shuffled inside and barred the door. He was a coward, and I knew he was afraid of the soldiers. He never opened his door again to Jeshua of Nazareth, nor willingly to me.

That night the rabbi slept in the empty stable with Thomas and a few others. The sheep had gone onto the mountain that past week. Toward midnight a man came, a spy named Judas ish Keriot. With him were two Roman soldiers carrying torches, and they searched the house. From my place in the store room, I watched the torchlight on the stone walls shudder and grow dim, and I was afraid my father would betray us. But then the soldiers went away. All was quiet, and in time my sister brought me some food. She stood beside the doorpost with her bruised face.

"Drunkards," she said. "They'll come again when it's light."

In the morning Thomas Didymus found us where we were working in the garden. He spoke to my sister—"This is the sign. At sunset you will meet a man carrying a jar of water, standing by the Fountain gate. Knock where he goes in. If a man stops you, ask for the upper room where they'll eat the feast."

She said, "Won't you come with us?"

"Our faces are known." Then, "Bargiona will send a man to walk with you, a stranger."

It was a sign of how little they cared for him, that they would leave him to be led by women. Already they thought of ways to save themselves. Pontius Pilate kept many spies. Judas ish Keriot was one of many in the town.

I judge them cruelly, but they were right to be afraid. Later in the morning, the man Thaddeus slipped through the gate. He brought news to my father. Dimas and Gestas bar Sirach had been condemned by Pilate's magistrate. They would be crucified at Golgotha on the last day of preparation, before the sacrifices in the temple were to start. These were two friends of Judas Sicarius, taken by the guard on Solomon's porch when the rabbi was in the temple.

Our stable was beyond the bean field in a row of trees. Men slipped in and out during the morning, their cloaks over their heads.

We worked in the garden. In the middle of the day, Martha was in the house making food. But once I went back with a jug of water and found her on her knees, her hand pressed to her thick belly. There was blood under her nose and on her cheeks. I would have gone to her, only she scolded me and wouldn't let me touch her. She cursed me, and told me to take bread and lentils to the stables. She told me to say nothing to my father, but serve the men and not disgrace myself or her.

When I entered through the low door, I recognized Philip, Andrew, Bartholomew, Matthew, James, and his brother John, sitting in the shadows. They ate what I brought, filling their cheeks without thanking me. They licked their fingers without washing them. Now the rabbi's influence was less, they showed more of what they were, landless farmers from Galilee. Fisherman who had lost their boats. I was a rich man's daughter, who served them for the rabbi's sake.

Jeshua of Nazareth sat with them in the straw. Once he had said, "Among my friends are neither rich nor poor, man nor woman, slave nor free." I think only the poor, the women, and the slaves understood him. I knew I should be humble, but why should worthless fools be raised up?

He said, "God has turned his head. But I tell you the day is coming when the temple will burn. When Jerusalem is ringed by Caesar's armies, then you'll run away. Don't stop to take your clothes or anything you own, because there won't be time."

Philip said, "When will this happen?"

"Some of you will see. I tell you this, a rich man made a journey to a far country. He called his slaves and handed over money for them to keep. To one he gave five silver coins, another, three, and to the last he gave one copper penny. Then after a long time he came back for his money. The one who had a single penny said, I knew you were a cruel man, living from other people's work. I dug a hole. See here it is, and your penny at the bottom of it.

"So the rich man said, I will take this and give it to the others. You who have nothing deserve nothing. This useless slave, kill him and throw his body out the door."

I have heard Simon Bargiona and Saul of Tarsus explain this story. They said the rich man was the rabbi himself, gone to a far country and come back.

But I was there, and I think the rabbi was the last slave, whose trust had been so shaken. Maybe the first was Simon Peter himself, who had grown rich in the rabbi's service. Maybe the second was Philip of Bethsaida, who had bought a house in Sepphoris.

Philip got up scowling and slipped out through the break in the stone wall. Soon after, Thomas went with Mary of Magdala while the rabbi was still talking. She stood next to him with tears in her eyes, but he said nothing. At last Thomas beckoned to her, and she bent her head and left. Later he looked for her but she was gone.

Men who weren't there made up stories about what the rabbi said that day in our stable in Bethany, below the hill of Olives. The ruined temple, Jerusalem burned, Judaea conquered, everything has happened as he said. But he said nothing of the world's end or the day of judgment when the dead will rise. Maybe he was full of doubts. But now I pray for what comes without saying. How can it not be true at long last? The sun will be darkened, and the moon blotted out. The son of man will gather his followers from the four winds.

When the long shadows came down from the hill and covered the stable where we sat, I lit a lamp. But I had forgotten to fill it, and soon it guttered and went out. The rabbi smiled. But I was frightened to disappoint him, and I went back to the house to get some oil.

I called to my sister, but I couldn't find her in the house. I found her kneeling on my mat in a corner of the store room, beyond the jars of wine. She was angry when she saw me—"Go. Don't touch. What if they need you and you're not there?"

"You'll come with me," I said, frightened. There was blood on her palms. I went to her and reached out my hands, but she pushed them away.

"There. Go wash. Try to be good. No, don't cry."

And when I told her about the oil, she said, "Take my lamp. I don't want it."

I was crying, and I left her in the dark. I hid from my father and ran across the yard. I brought the lamp into the stable, and Jeshua smiled.

"You see you must be ready when your bridegroom comes, ready for your own death or the world's end. Not for my sake, for the lamp is yours."

Yes, I'm watchful, as he told me. Everything that happened in those days, I seem to see them as if painted on a wall. Soon after, Matthew and Bartholomew slipped out through the door and made their own way to the town. The sons of thunder were already gone, and I was left alone with the rabbi. But I wouldn't let him see my face, because I was crying for my sister's sake. He had his own thoughts. He sat cross-legged in the lamplight, and I stood near him in the shadow, wondering what I should do, but not for long.

A man I'd never seen before was standing outside the door. He was a big man. He carried a hoe. He said nothing, but just stood there. I put out the lamp, picked up my sister's basket and went out into the evening. Jeshua followed me, and the man led us to the road, which was full of people hurrying to the gates. They were trying to reach it before nightfall. No one looked at us, though there were soldiers in the crowd.

The rabbi walked with his face uncovered, and no one looked at him. When we came to the Kidron, we crossed it and turned south along the ravine under the temple walls, and past the spring that flows through the mountain into Siloam pool. The valley was already full of shadow. High above on the red wall, soldiers were lighting watch fires along Solomon's porch.

The man walked in front, his hoe over his shoulder. Then came the rabbi, twenty paces behind, and I followed him. I came quick on his heels, because I was frightened of the dark. I heard the labor of his breath. I heard words of what I thought was a small prayer, repeated over and over. Then the rhythm of his breathing broke apart. I was following close behind, and I reached out my hand to touch his sleeve. He turned back, and I could see no tears on his face. Instead he was smiling. He stopped in the middle of the path, and for a moment he put his hands around my shoulders as if he were adjusting my cloak. He bent down and murmured, "Will you come with me?" I smelt his breath. When I said nothing, he continued: "Will you take my mother to stay in Lazarus's house?" It was as if he knew Simon the leper would soon be dead.

There was no wind, and as we came close to the Fountain gate, we saw the smoke from the dung fires rising from Ge-hinnon into the soft sky. All around us among the graves and ruined stones, country people had pitched their tents. Fires were burning at the gate, and in the crowd of beggars, inside the right-hand pillar of the inner door, a man waited. Nor could I have missed him, because I had never seen a man carrying a water jug, which was women's work. When he saw us he stepped into the road. Almost out of sight among the crowds, he led us through the lower city among the tiny streets, the markets of the tanners and the butchers and the pot makers. All around us the air stank with the smell of garbage and wet gutters, the dung fires and the burnt sacrifice that came down from the temple and filled the houses of the poor. I wrapped my shawl over my nose, but still my eyes hurt from the smoke out of every courtyard. Men sat on the rooftops eating lentils and roast meal. When they saw us they called out, for there was not an-other woman in the streets.

Each year at passover and tabernacles, the city was full of homeless beggars. Many of the rich went down to Jericho to escape the crowds. We climbed the narrow steps until we reached the valley of the cheese makers and the better markets. I didn't know the way. I could see big-ger houses above me on the west side of the Camel's Hump, and to my left on the ramparts of the upper town. We turned into the open mar-ket, the Xystus below the temple, which was full of people from the country selling vegetables and fruit and linen cloth, their blankets stretched out on the stones. Whole families were wrapped in blankets, because the night was cold. I saw soldiers, too, walking among the torches and the lamps.

Past Herod's empty theater rose the causeway and the aqueduct, and Herod's wall. Now we climbed the steep steps to the upper town. I'd never seen these places, the great streets by the Hasmonaean pal-ace. Above us rose Herod's towers, their tops still touched with red. But when the light left the sky, we stood outside a rich house in a nar-row, empty street.

We saw the man with the water jug standing on the threshold as we turned the corner. When we came to the house, we found the door was shut. Our other guide, the man who had come with us from Bethany, didn't wait. He walked down the street without turning and without a word, his hoe over his shoulder.

I knocked on the big door, and then we waited. The rabbi said noth-ing. He rubbed his hands together because the air was damp and cold.

Then we were let inside a cold house filled with men. The one who had unbarred the door took us to the courtyard. There was no comfort in the stone rooms, but only the smell of dirt and water. Men slept on the floor, curled in dirty straw.

Among the rabbi's students were two men named Simon. The sec-ond one, Simon the zealot, now came to the rail of the upper gallery. He looked down from the top of the ladder. "You see it's Cleopas's whore. Where's her sister? The whore can rake the fire."

This man had lost most of his teeth, though he was still young. His hair was full of lice. His father was a beggar who had lost his land. But the son wasn't content to work small jobs and drink his wages. He had plenty of money now, like most of the rabbi's students. He opened his shirt and pulled his purse from his neck. He threw some coins into the courtyard where they clattered in the dirt at my feet.

They were lighting lamps now that night was come. On the gallery above us I could see a table. Men lay on couches: Simon Bargiona and his brother, Philip of Bethsaida, Bartholomew, and the sons of Zebedee. I caught glimpses of them through the posts of the rail.

I put my basket down. Always I asked myself what my sister would do. That night especially I thought of her as I shoveled out the ashes from the pit. I raked out the smoking charcoal and laid the fire.

There was an Egyptian girl, a slave of the householder. Later she came to live with us in Bethany. That night she brought water from the big jar. She bent to take the money Simon had thrown down. I wanted to go with her when she went out the door, but instead I took my comfort from the rabbi, as my sister would have wanted.

Jeshua of Nazareth stood at the bottom of the ladder, where one or two came to ask his blessing and show their wounds. He couldn't see me as I squatted on the stones, because soon I had gathered my own circle of men. Five or six stood around me or else squatted down, staring at my face, following every motion of my hands. When I pushed my sleeve up, I heard one of them clear his throat. I looked at him. It was Thaddeus the zealot. There was a golden color in his beard. As I watched him, he knelt down beside me. His eyes never blinked.

I was frightened and pulled down my sleeve, feeling my weakness among these men. Then there was a noise from the door, and Judas Sicarius came into the courtyard. He was to have married me. As he threw his cloak over his shoulder, I could see the sword at his belt. With him came Thomas, Matthew the toll collector, and Jacob, who was the rabbi's brother. I was happy to see them, especially Thomas Didymus. They walked past me to the ladder's foot where Jeshua of Nazareth stood.

Of all men he was the easiest to know. Nor could he hide his anger—"Is this what I told you?" He came toward Judas, his hand raised.

He was talking about their weapons. He said, "You've made your way. Now if you find yourself without a sword, sell your coat and buy one."

Matthew opened his shirt—"Here are two swords."

Jeshua said, "Enough. Tomorrow everything men say will be the truth. But I tell you tonight for the last time—"

His voice was low and soft and fast, as if he muttered to himself. Above him I could see Simon Bargiona at the gallery rail, his arms and thick legs splayed as he leaned over us. The lamplight shone on his bald head. "If you give up, that's your choice. Some of us will fight. You weren't with us yesterday at Siloam's Pool."

Judas Sicarius moved away, and was talking to other men in the courtyard. After they spoke to him, they put on their coats and gathered up their things. I watched them, but I was listening to the rabbi. He said, "With us the strongest was the weakest. Simon Bargiona, do you understand?"

The fat man tried to speak but Jeshua interrupted him—"Satan loves you. But I want you to be strong and to strengthen these others."

I was surprised to see tears in Bargiona's eyes— "Lord, I would have gone to prison. I would have died for you."

All this time the men sat around me, staring as I moved my hands, pushed my hair back from my face. And Thaddeus the zealot knelt beside me, staring as I rolled out the flat bread, the dough mixed from flour and water, which I had brought in my sister's basket. My cheeks were hot. I brushed the dough with oil and laid it on the hot bronze plate.

Nothing Jeshua said had made these men turn their heads. But now Judas Sicarius came back to the bottom of the ladder. "We'll fight about this elsewhere if we can. Pilate knows about this house."

There was a moment of quiet in the courtyard and the hall. The men around me got up slowly, and in the rooms they were stumbling to their feet. Then there were others, even the wounded, who got up and took their things, calling to each other. They unbarred the door. There was a back door, too, and as time went on the men went slinking out. They pushed past the African slave as she came in carrying a wine jar. She stepped into the confusion of the courtyard, and I rose to meet her. I walked into a ring of quiet that surrounded my lord.

Judas Sicarius said, "Rabbi, let me go."

Jeshua answered, "Here is Mary, who has brought supper."

"Lord," I said, "there's nothing here."

Jeshua laughed. "Then you'll make something out of nothing. Give us wine and the flat bread, because these men are eager to be gone. Perhaps the danger will fly over us."

Judas said, "There is no time."

Now we were left alone. I went back and squatted by the fire. The zealots were departing, and the man Thaddeus was gone, although I looked for him. The circle of quiet around the rabbi grew until the court was empty, except for his students. Those who had been at the table upstairs came down the ladder, and they stood at the ladder's foot while Jeshua walked toward me. I bent down over the fire pit. He came to warm his hands as I laid the bread out on the hearth.

As he came close beside me, I remembered my dirty hands. "What's in the pot?" he asked.

"Hot water."

He knelt and dipped a cloth into it. Then he turned back and said, "Come, let us say a prayer." When no one moved, he brought the towel to them, Philip and Andrew and some others. When he came to Judas Sicarius, he paused. He reached out with the cloth.

"Rabbi, you won't wash my hands," Sicarius said.

Then: "Lord, you will not," he repeated, and put up his palms. "I swear to you, there's no time for these games." When Jeshua did nothing, he leaned forward and kissed him on the chin and would have held him, except the rabbi stepped back.

"Go quickly," he said.

Judas Sicarius turned his head and walked away. His sandals made a clatter on the stones. With him went Matthew, Bartholomew, and Simon the zealot, and the rabbi watched them go.

Andrew said, "If you wash my hands, why not my feet?"

Jeshua smiled. He made these things a lesson. But those men had no shame. They were treacherous men from Galilee, and I served them. At that moment I felt closest to my lord. He came toward me, smiling. He took the bread from my hands and brought it to them, saying a prayer. Some were already out the door and some refused. I saw John and James of Zebedee, the sons of thunder, the rabbi's cousins, take one of the flat loaves.

I imagined I was polluting them with everything I touched. I filtered out a cup of wine, mixed it with water, and the rabbi took it. He raised it up. "Don't deny me this," he said.

James, and John, and Thomas Didymus each took the cup and drank. But Simon Bargiona was gone. With him went Andrew, Philip, and Jacob of Alpheus. They had left the courtyard when we heard a pounding on the door and then a voice called, "Where's your brother? Where've you left him?"

It was the rabbi's mother. Now we saw her in the doorway. She had Jacob by the shirt. She was holding him with both hands by the front of his shirt, and he was pulling away. She was a tall woman as I said, taller than her second son. Maybe his father was small, like most Greeks.

He pulled away and she cursed him. He was gone out the door and she came toward us. She said, "There's soldiers in the streets."

And Jeshua—"Woman, what are you doing? This is not the place for you."

But she came toward us, toward the fire pit. Her big feet were splashed with mud. Maybe she'd drunk beer or wine.

She held up her crooked fingers, worn with work. She held up her palms. "What have you done?" she said. Her voice was clumsy, because of her anger. "Herod Antipas is in the town. Joanna spoke to her husband, who will speak for you. Pontius Pilate is not your governor. Herod Antipas is king over the Galileans."

The rabbi shrugged his shoulders. His mother reached for him, but he stepped back. "Then I beg you," she said, clasping her hands together. "Your brothers are there, your young sister."

He said, "I'm with my family now."

She raised her hands, knotted into fists. "This is your family? Murderers and thieves. Fool!" she said, and then other curses which she shouted, tears on her face. Jeshua turned away and left her. With the others he went out by the back door, and I went with them.

He walked quickly through the streets. I think he was following a ghost, because he needed none of us to find the way, though it was black night. He led us past the market, and we hurried to keep up. The gate was closed, but the postern was still open. Jeshua walked past the guard and down into the valley, speaking to no one. "Lord," said

Thomas Didymus, "we can't take this road. They will look for us in Bethany." But the rabbi walked ahead into the dark, singing a small song.

He kept on until the Gesthemene wall, where Solomon had kept his wine press. It was near the fig tree where I sat with him the day before. Maybe he saw it looming in the darkness, but he turned and stood in the middle of the road as we came up. The sons of thunder, John and James of Zebedee, were there. "Lord," said John, "Ish Keriot is close behind."

We stood in the quiet road, waiting. I squatted in the dust. Few travelers passed by. Behind us we saw torchlight. We heard the small clamor of soldiers, the jingle of their weapons, their small cries. Around us the dark night, the squeaking bats. I squatted in the cold road, listening to the soldiers. "No," said James. But Jeshua of Nazareth stood in the middle of the road.

There was a Roman decurion on horseback. We saw him now with the torches around him. The rabbi said, "This is far enough."

As he was talking, Thomas Didymus ran into the garden, away under the trees. James of Zebedee walked up the road till he was out of sight. John stayed behind. I squatted in the dust and watched the Romans coming. I heard their laughing voices.

"John," he said, "go now. This woman will stay with me." But John did nothing. In his young face, now that the torches were near, I could see a suffering. Maybe like the rabbi he was looking for a sign. Still he did nothing when Jeshua turned from us and walked back down the road.

Then we saw Ish Keriot, a bald man under the torches. He ran toward us—"There he is." Soldiers were coming, and the decurion on his gray horse. But Jeshua stood in the middle of the road.

"And the son of Zebedee," shouted Judas ish Keriot. He ran past me where I squatted in the road. The soldiers held Jeshua with his arms behind him. He made no move to throw them off. But John took a knife from his shirt, one of the curved sicae the zealots carried. When Ish Keriot grabbed him by his cloak, he put the knife into the spy's neck, then jumped back to the shadow by the wall. He climbed up and was gone. Two soldiers chased him.

Judas ish Keriot sat down crying as the blood ran from his neck. I saw Jeshua in the circle of torchlight. The soldiers dragged him back, holding his arms together. But I thought he could do nothing for the spy, who lay down on his side in the road.

The Romans made no move to help him, though he cried out. The decurion got off his horse and stood over him, talking with another soldier in words I didn't know.

The decurion took off his leather cap. He ran his fingers over his clipped head. He was waiting for the soldiers who chased John. When they climbed back empty-handed over the wall, he called to them. He never looked at me. I crouched in the dry sand near the ditch while he stood talking to his men. Then he took his horse and walked back toward the town. I watched the soldiers follow, leading Jeshua of Nazareth between them.

The moon rose, and by its light I could see the face of Judas ish Keriot, his cheek pressed to the road. John's linen cloak lay over the dead man's legs. Blood had gathered in the dust near his head, and he was bleeding from a cut on his right ear. He was a small man.

He was a spy for Pontius Pilate and the high priests. Though a Jew, he cared nothing for our Jewish law. Still, maybe I should have done better than just leave him without a word or prayer, leave his ghost to wander. Every man needs a woman to cry over him, as my sister once said. I stood in the moonlight by the road. I thought at least I should drag the body to the ditch. I thought that's what my sister would have done. But I was too frightened to touch it, so I left it for the pigs and the wild dogs. When I passed by in the morning there was nothing, just a trampled place in the dry dirt.

* * *

I went on to Bethany, keeping to the darkness. When I knocked on my father's door, he didn't answer for a long time. Then I heard the sound of his shuffling and the bar drawing back. He stood leaning on his stick. The lamp was behind him on an overturned basket. I saw the outline of his crooked body, his big head.

He cursed at me as was his habit. But he didn't move aside. He

70

wouldn't let me cross the threshold to the big room. He called me a whore for Jeshua of Nazareth, whose mother was a whore. He told me to find Jeshua of Nazareth, because he was the king of Israel and would protect me.

After he closed the door and bolted it, I stood in the courtyard by the sycamore tree. Later I went to the empty stable. I wrapped myself in straw. But then I heard my sister calling from my brother's window. I could see a light moving back and forth along the sill. I walked over the packed dirt of the kitchen yard, and she brought me quietly into the room. She put the lamp on the sill. By its light I could see the marks across her face. One eye was partly closed.

I couldn't find the words to ask her what had happened. Nor could I tell her. She said nothing, only stared at me out of her eye. Her hands weren't gentle as she helped me down. She said nothing and was eager to go. But I saw a tray of food inside the wool curtain, which blocked the door into the house. I smelled it, along with the smells of my brother's body. When she was gone through the curtain, I sat down on the hard dirt.

She'd made food of a kind I'd never tasted. Always before I'd eaten lentils and locust shells, dry porridge and flat beans. I'd drunk only water, or goat's milk mixed with water. But on the tray I found my father's glass cup full of wine. I found pieces of cold lamb and honey bread, dates from Jericho and the green figs. I found a bowl of walnuts and cucumber.

Sitting in a corner of the wall, out of sight of my brother's eyes, I washed my hands in water and gave thanks. But with all that food, there was a sickness in my stomach when I thought about myself, or my sister, or Thaddeus the zealot, or Jeshua of Nazareth.

I took a mouthful of wine and swallowed it. I thought my brother's smell would make me sick. To forget myself, I took the lamp and stood over him where he lay on the straw bed. He hadn't moved since I came in. I thought he was asleep. But now I saw his eyes were open, watching me, following the lamp. He lay naked in his dirt. His man's part was stiff and swollen. My father had chained him to the wall with a long chain, joined to a leather cuff around his ankle.

I thought of the rabbi in the Antonia fortress, in Pilate's cell. But I bent over my brother with the lamp in my hand. A bucket of dirt stood by his bed, a pool of water on the floor. I lowered the bucket out the window to the ground, and the rest of that hour I spent washing Lazarus. With handfuls of rushes from the bed, I mopped my brother's water. I washed his legs with wet linen. I hoped he wouldn't cry and wake my father. But he lay without moving, his breath quiet as I wrapped him in bed sheets to hide his nakedness. His eyes followed me in everything I did.

Then he raised himself up and tried to speak. The spit fell from his mouth. He was shaking his head back and forth. I felt no threat of danger, but only the division from myself that is the fate of women. As I soothed him, I saw my hands as if they were another's.

Later I sat by the lamp in a corner of the wall. Now when I took bites of the food my sister had prepared, I savored it, and I drank all the wine. There were other gifts: a purse of coins, which I slipped into my belt. An amulet for luck: some words of the law written on sheep skin, which my sister had wrapped around a locust's egg, a fox's tooth, and a gallows nail. She had tied them up with string in a small bundle, and the string went around my neck. I sat clutching it and didn't sleep.

Early in the morning I climbed into the yard and wrapped my cloth around my face. I stole a jar from the barn and went out the gate, hoping men would think I was about my business at the well. But when they passed me on the road, I stepped into the ditch. I touched my fist to my forehead, as I'd seen servants do.

I scarcely knew where I was going. Now I am ashamed to think I was so foolish, though I was already a woman—twelve years old. But I had an idea that I would find Thaddeus the zealot in the house in the upper town. I would tell him what had happened. Or else find the rabbi's mother . . .

These were the days of preparation for the feast. When I reached the main road, even at first light it was full of people. Shepherds whistled to the new white lambs, and men drove donkeys and camels. Among so many strangers I moved faster. Women carried hens in wicker cages.

Some had families in the lower town. Some rented places in the stables and courtyards of the Tyropoeon. Most of the rest were camped outside the wall, in the Kidron valley near the spring. They'd put their tents around the ruined arch, the tomb of Absalom. I'd seen them when I passed with Jeshua of Nazareth the day before. Now there were twice as many and the road smelled of their smoke. Children played in the ditches while their parents scavenged for wood.

There was a mass of people at the gate around the toll collectors. Some had money and went through. The rest stayed back until the crowd was big enough and the collectors couldn't keep us out. I stood in the crowd and from time to time we would press forward. I heard the ugly accent of the Galileans. The feast had brought the country people to Jerusalem. A man pulled at my shawl and muttered under his breath. He smelled of onions. When we passed under the double gate it was no better. He followed me, muttering curses and pulling the tuft of his red beard. After a while he stopped and let me go.

The rocks opened a cut on my right heel. I pushed through the crowd, climbed through the huts until I reached the stone steps to the upper town. In the grand streets near the Hasmonaean palace I went looking for the house of Joanna's husband, who was Herod's servant. I thought perhaps the rabbi's mother stayed there. But before I found it I saw Mary of Magdala outside the council house.

This house was a square building under a flat roof, held up by columns of ridged stone. Greeks had built it for Herod the king. Mary was sitting in the crowd on the big stairs. When I saw her, for the first time I knew Jeshua of Nazareth would die. Not because she screamed and wailed. Her bare face was calm, but like a corpse's, streaked with the white dust she had rubbed over her hair. She sat with her knees drawn up.

Some Galilean women stood above her, talking. I saw Zebedee's wife, Salome of Capernaum, wiping her big face. But I said nothing to her, and no one spoke to me as I looked up toward the doors. Jeshua of Nazareth was one of many that the Romans had arrested during the night.

In this house, I imagined, the high priest Caiaphas, his wife's father, Annas, and the rest of the sanhedrin sat in the stone chairs or walked among the columns. In my mind I made a picture of the priests inside, whom I'd seen at the processions when I was a girl. Some were Roman citizens and wore the Roman clothes. Others kept the long beards and old hats of the sadducees, but they were all the same, rich men chosen by Pontius Pilate to do his work.

I sat on the stone steps, looking south over the roofs to the south wall, the fog over the Dung gate. Around me the air smelled of slaughtered animals. Men came to these streets from all over the world. There was no room for them.

On my right hand the upper market spread among the houses. Beyond it I could see the red walls of the Hasmonaean palace. Beyond them, the three towers of Hippicus. I was tired, and might have fallen asleep on the stone steps because of the wine I'd drunk. But then the small door opened above me and a man was there, a servant of the council. His name was Asterius Agrippa, a Jew. He was dressed in the Roman style, and his legs were bare.

I stood up as the crowd gathered around me. But I was close enough to hear him speak the names of the men Pontius Pilate had condemned, as he did on the fifth day of every week. When he got to Jeshua of Nazareth, he paused. He asked if anyone there knew the bandits Simon the fisherman, called Bargiona, and Simon the zealot, and Judas called Sicarius.

Asterius Agrippa was a rich man who cared nothing for the poor. "Now," he said, "there's something else. The magistrate has put up thirty silver drachmae, Judas of Keriot's wages, who died last night on the Bethany road. He has no family, and I'll pay the money for the sake of the feast. Anyone who knows these bandits—"

I could scarcely hear him. Since the time he spoke the names of those who would be crucified, women had cried out. Three who stood near me started wailing. Then they sank to their knees on the smooth steps.

Over them I saw the rabbi's mother. All this time I hadn't recognized her, as she'd stood with the cloth over her head. Now she stripped it away to show her long, coarse face—she had no tears. Instead she raised her fists to heaven as she cursed. "Hypocrites, sons of whores," she shouted, the same words Jeshua had spoken. "Pilate's shit stools, shit on his boots," and other things before the men took her by the arms. "I know Simon Bargiona," she said. "That bald pig. Let me tell you—" But they wouldn't listen, because she was a woman.

Later I heard she went back to claim the money. But now I walked behind her as the men took her down the steps. The crowd parted. When I looked back, I saw Asterius Agrippa on the open step under the high portico, his small beard, his bordered shirt, his gold rings and collar, his bare knees. Seeing him, I was ashamed to be a woman. I lowered my eyes, shut my ears to the noise of the crowd. I know the rabbi's mother felt no shame, but my cheeks burned.

* * *

It was a custom since Annius Rufus's time for the Romans to release a Jew from prison in honor of the passover. So that day Jeshua Barabbas was released. He had been a leader of the Galilean zealots, and once his men had attacked the Roman prison in Caesarea, during the passover when I was just a girl. Many loved him for his bravery, and they gathered in front of the Antonia gate to welcome him. But when the soldiers brought him out, the crowd fell silent.

Pilate had blinded him, cut off his nose, his ears, his hands and feet. The Romans carried him out and threw him down onto the stones. They left him crawling naked on his knees, and no one came to help him. Then his sister and her servants brought him to her husband's house.

In time we all got used to him lying on a mat inside the temple by the Beautiful gate, begging for food and money. He lived there for years. He grew fat. I remember him sitting, rocking on his knees, singing, "Barabbas is my name." Or, "Give me a silver penny, for I fought against the Romans."

I knew nothing about this until later. The day he was released, I was with Mary of Magdala. I followed Jeshua's mother when she left the council house, but then I lost her in the crowd.

I wanted to be with her, but in a moment she was gone. Men stood in my way, and I looked back and saw Mary of Magdala on the lower stairs. Not knowing where to go, I went and sat beside her, hugging my knees as she did. Sometimes I tried to catch her eyes. She was beautiful that morning, her copper-colored curls, her white skin. Or in my weakness she seemed that way, though her dress was plain, her cheeks streaked with dirt. I wanted her to speak to me but she said nothing even when I began to cry. I put my face into my hands.

Jeshua's mother, I knew, would have put her arms around me. But there's a comfort in silence, too, because my tears dried after a while. I sat hugging my knees, and my head was empty. In time I felt a finger on my shoulder. Mary of Magdala had gotten to her feet.

She touched me with her finger as she got up. She covered her head and stepped into the dirty street. She stepped through the soldiers down into the crowd, and I followed her. Having no place to go, not knowing what to do, I followed her into the lower town. She slipped through the crowds, but I felt men all around me. I couldn't walk as fast, but I kept sight of her in front of me. I stumbled down the wide stone steps into the valley of the lower town, following the wine-red woolen shawl that was like all the virgin of Magdala's clothes—dirty and worn, though once rich. I thought there was something in the way she walked and spoke that kept her apart out of the crowd, protected her and made us all remember she was a rich man's daughter, no matter where she lived or what she did. Now in the lower markets she moved quickly through the drunken men, her bare feet dry. Mine were covered with the shit and mud.

Alone among women, I thought, she had the skill to do whatever she wanted. After the rabbi's death, she lived by herself in a cave in the red rocks, the Blood Ascent in the Judaean desert. No one harmed her. Later still she was a whore on the world's roads and even crossed the sea to Alexandria, or so I heard. I didn't doubt it. That day she led me to places I'd never been, would never see again. She led me to the public fountain, which Pontius Pilate had built out of the aqueduct. Women beat the clumps of wet clothes on the open stones, and the gutters ran with dye. Boys stood under the brimming stones, naked but for rags around their thighs, though it was a cold, foggy day. These were the streets built into the narrow valleys below the ramparts of Mount Zion, deep in shadow, smelling of fuller's dirt and soaking hides.

Mary of Magdala unwound her shawl and put it aside. There was no place for a woman to wash herself here, but still she tucked her dress into her belt and pushed up her sleeves. If I had done that, the men would have shouted and thrown stones, but she stood among the boys below the lip of the pool. She washed her head and face, her arms and feet. I thought she was protected by the evil eye. Or maybe the men and women knew her. She came often to these poor places, and the rabbi had come too.

She had some nitre folded in a reed. It made a froth on her hands and feet when she was washing them. I stood with other women in the gutter, squatting to rub away the crust between my toes. I felt humble and dirty, watching her pour out water in a public cup, letting the drops fall between her fingers and then holding the cup above her head, giving thanks.

Her red shawl lay on the stones. No one had touched it. I went and squatted nearby, so she would see me when she came back. I had an offering which I bought from a man next to the pool, a honey cake wrapped in grass. Mary came toward me, shaking out her hair, wiping her face with her fingers, smiling, and I thought she was happy. Though the rabbi was in prison, she was happy. Though she must have known I'd followed her from the council steps, she looked at me as if for the first time. She smiled and held out her hands, and when I pressed the honey cake into it, she said no prayer. She brought the cake up to her nose and smelled it, then laughed as she thrust it into her mouth. I didn't expect her to eat in front of the men and boys, to swallow the cake in one bite without letting go of my hand. She didn't hide her mouth. She held my hand in her right hand, pinching the skin between my forefinger and thumb. When I tried to pull away, she put her other hand into my belt, searching there until she found the rag full of coins my sister gave me. All this time I was looking into her gray eyes, which were set askew, the left one wandering. I thought this was her mark, the one that filled me with envy and pity. The one that let her move through the crowd, wash in the open street, cross the threshold into my father's house, though she had no husband. The mark that let her strike a man across the face. She took my money out of my rope belt, the coins my sister Martha had stolen or saved, and I let her do it. Her face was close to mine. Her eyes were level with my eyes, though she was older than me, past the age of marriage, maybe eighteen years old.

She wrapped her shawl around her head and walked over the wet stones, down through the bottom of the valley, through the poor streets and dead ends where the weavers' children picked at the wet flax, the day laborers waited and drank. We walked down among the stone pits where the fullers soaked their wool, the small streets under the south wall, and when we got to the Dung gates, Mary turned. With my money clenched between her fingers, she shook her fist at the rich houses on the Camel's Hump, the pinnacle of the temple on the mountain above it, and we could hear the trumpets, smell the bloody smoke.

The gates were empty except for the soldiers. Beyond, the slope led down into the valley of Ge-hinnon, where no man wants to go. All the garbage of the city flowed through the culverts underneath the wall, or else was carried out in dripping carts to the ravine where the fires burned.

I followed Mary of Magdala. Our feet broke through the crusted sand. Children called to us as we came down into the ravine, held out their hands. But Mary was smiling, and I could see they knew her. They led us in among the mud houses, whose walls were decorated with red hand prints and the drying cakes of winnowed dung.

There was an open circle in the middle of that village in Ge-hinnon. We stopped there to catch our breath, surrounded by a circle of children. Their mothers stood apart, and I was looking at their faces, because I had never seen such women. Their heads were bare, their foreheads and chins and the backs of their hands covered with red tattoos. They had no understanding of the law which forbids these things. They had metal rings in their ears, metal plugs thrust through their nostrils and the centers of their ears. I saw lepers among them—not like my father, just in name.

A blind old woman came forward, leaning on a stick. She struggled through the sand, then reached up with her dirty fingers to touch Mary's face. Afterward she came to me, but I pushed her away. I was angry, because Mary of Magdala gave my money to that old woman. Later she told me she had bought a knife.

The wind had stirred the sand under our feet. Toothless, the old woman was muttering about Jeshua of Nazareth, and for the first time I thought the rabbi had been here. I couldn't bear the sight of her blind eyes. She thrust my money into the front of her dress, which I could see was full of other purses.

We spent the day and the night too. In time the older children and the men came back from begging and stealing in the town. As evening fell they built a fire of thorn trees, and in the darkness they brought out basins of unfiltered wine.

There was a cold dusty wind out of the desert, which made the sparks fly. I sat with a baby on my lap. He was awake and crying softly. Mary of Magdala stood with her hands on her hips, her copper-colored hair around her shoulders, her face red with wine and the flickering light. She wore no bracelets or rings. Her shawl was trampled in the sand.

The boys were seeing who could jump the highest as the fire jumped up. Or they snatched the glowing brands out of the pit and ran away, until all we saw were the red circles as they swung the brands around their heads. The smoke blew all around us.

That day, I found out later, Jeshua's mother went to Herod's palace where the governor stayed when he was in Jerusalem. She'd heard that Claudia Procula, the governor's wife, sometimes came out in the afternoon to breathe the air, and was carried in a litter through the upper town. She thought she would beg for mercy before Pilate's wife. She joined a group of women who were always there, whether the litter came out or not. But she didn't call out from a distance like the others. Nor did she weep or tear her hair. But she ran forward when the litter was at the Mariamne gate, and she pushed through the soldiers when Claudia Procula came out, when the steward brought the ladder and she was ready to climb up. I heard the tyrant's wife was veiled in silk with no part of her skin exposed, a tiny woman standing among the soldiers of the guard—yellow-haired men, tall and strong. But Jeshua's mother pushed through them and went down into the dust, holding Claudia Procula's ankles as she begged for her son's life, dust in her hair, her face white with dust. The soldiers would have thrown her out, kicked her away, except Claudia Procula spoke a word to make them wait.

* * *

We slept in the sand around the glowing fire. When Mary of Magdala woke me it was not yet dawn. But she touched me on the shoulder and I sat up under the dark sky, the pale stars. My hair was full of sand. My cheeks were tender, bruised. I followed Mary down to the stream, and among the piles of dung I washed my hands and eyes. I saw Mary wrap her shawl over her head, around her face. I did the same. Then we walked up through the sand, through the wide ravine up to the city.

That morning there was a crowd around the gate, because the toll collectors were there. We stood on a jutting rock, watching the sky grow red behind the hill of Olives, beyond the narrow valley. Even in the chill of morning we could feel the promise of a hot, cloudless day, almost the first of the year, which had been cold and wet. We stood watching a crowd of pilgrims come up from the lower ford over the Kidron, the men loud and excited, the young men hand in hand. Others came from the city gate with small pots of water from Siloam. They passed us, looking for places to squat on the rough slopes above Ge-hinnon.

We heard the trumpets behind the red walls. Still there was no movement. Men stood in groups, or else they wandered off alone, looking for clean places. I followed Mary's finger, and we climbed up the slope to find two of the rabbi's students—Matthew, and Thaddeus the zealot. The beautiful man. They sat across from each other in a sandy place near where the drains came out under the wall. There was a bitter smell and many flies, still sluggish, crawling on the rocks.

They didn't recognize us until we stood above them, and Mary spoke. They looked up for a moment, and Thaddeus the zealot didn't look at me. He went back to staring at the dry dirt between his feet, mumbling his words, but no, they wouldn't go see Jeshua of Nazareth die that day.

They didn't want to talk. What they said, Mary goaded out of them, I don't remember how. But she must have called them hypocrites and cowards, because Thaddeus glanced up, angry—Jeshua was the liar. He deserved to die.

The more they trusted him to chase out Herod and the Romans, the more they hated him now. And us. "You women are whores," Thaddeus said, which was so cruel. At that moment I knew he was a bad man, and promised myself not to think about him. I was to break that promise.

"You are whores," he said again. This was the heart of it, we found out later. On the third day of the week, the zealots had attacked the temple and the soldiers at Siloam. Dimas bar Sirach and Gestas were taken, but the rest escaped, beaten and shamed. When they gathered in the upper town, Simon Bargiona told them about the rabbi's mother. He said her first husband was a carpenter named Joseph. But he put her away and wouldn't touch her, because when they were married she was already pregnant with Jeshua of Nazareth. Simon Bargiona knew who the father was, a Syrian, a soldier from the twelfth legion.

"You have defeated us," Thaddeus went on. He was a tanner's son from Galilee, and God knows what impurity had put that tinge of gold into his hair. Magdala explained what he was saying as we skirted the wall.

"If women are corrupt, then God will punish men." Though I had spent a day and night with her, I think these were her first words to me.

We climbed down to the road and followed it west under the wall. We came into the city through the Valley gate. Inside, the streets were full of pilgrims. Above us on the hills we could see the empty houses of the rich, who had taken their slaves and wives down to Jericho.

We passed under the aqueduct, then along the old racecourse which Herod never finished. We went through the break in Herod's wall. In the open square before the gate of the Antonia, we stood waiting with the others for the prisoners to come out.

I recognized one or two out of the crowd. The rabbi's mother was there, and her cousin Salome, the wife of Zebedee, mother of James and John. I think we were the only ones there for Jeshua's sake. The rest—it was Pilate's day of execution, the sixth day of the week. Beggars and bandits—fourteen men were crucified that day. Soldiers led them out across the open stones. They were naked without even a rag. Each man had his ankles shackled with a heavy rope. The soldiers had beaten them. One man's legs were streaked with blood.

Now it was bright day. The sun was rising over the hill of Olives, over the walls of the temple into the clear sky. Dust settled on the stones. The light was all around us, the sky blue and dark. It was the second hour of the morning. Already I was sweating in my clothes.

Mary of Magdala pushed through the crowd. No one spoke. I saw many women—mothers, wives, sisters. The rest were people from the streets, happy to see justice and a painful death. I stood holding the amulet around my neck, the gallows nail, the fox's tooth, the locust's egg, which my sister had given me. I stood in the first row. For a moment everyone was quiet. We could hear the tramp of the soldiers' boots, the shouts of the decurion. His yellow hair shone in the sun.

The group of prisoners broke apart, and in the middle I could see the rabbi. He was bigger, taller than the rest. I saw his nakedness, his body, his broad chest covered with hair. I saw the wounds on his shoulders, the bruises on his face. And his hair clipped short, his beard scraped short—the others had long hair and wild beards. They were starving, broken men. They shuffled stupidly, or wept, or hid their faces. But he stood with his legs spread, looking at the sky. Then he lowered his head to find us in the crowd. Or rather Mary of Magdala. I could see him searching for her. Then she unwound the red shawl from her head until her face was bare. She shook her head, and her hair, which had been twisted up, fell down.

I looked for Gestas and Dimas bar Sirach, but couldn't tell them from the rest of those thieves. But there was another man called Simon, a famous murderer who killed a woman in Jericho. He was a Greek slave from Cyrene, who had accepted circumcision and then taken a Jewish name. He had two sons by a Jewish woman. Many of the crowd had come to see him die. When the decurion spoke his name, they shouted and threw stones. He was a small man with a swollen face, a wound on his forehead.

The men stayed against the wall with the crowd in a half circle. The soldiers kept us back from them. Now the silence was broken, and I was surrounded by angry shouts. I couldn't hear the decurion when he spoke. No one cared about Jeshua of Nazareth. It was Simon they had come to see, but he fell to the ground behind Jeshua and covered himself up. People were throwing stones and garbage. I was afraid they would hit the rabbi, because of all the men he was the only one who stood and faced the crowd. He was staring at Mary of Magdala. I saw no sadness or shame in him. Only hunger, I thought.

There was a pile of wooden beams against the wall, each the height of a man. These were the cross pieces for the gallows. It was the custom for the men to carry them along the street up to the Gennath gate, to

Golgotha. That way the market crowds would punish them as they came through.

Now the decurion raised his hand. The soldiers came around the prisoners and whipped them toward the beams, which were filthy with blood, used many times. The soldiers stood over Simon and whipped him, because he was too weak to lift his beam. But then Jeshua spoke. He lifted up his beam and Simon's too, balancing them across his body, clasping them in his big arms.

He was the first into the crowd, which parted in front of him, out of reach of the swinging beams. The others followed. They took small steps because of the ropes between their ankles. They carried their beams on their bowed backs, or else across their shoulders. Only Jeshua held his in his arms. He was the only one to walk upright. The others staggered after him and the soldiers followed, prodding their legs with the blunt ends of their spears while the boys ran alongside. Then came the crowd, which grew thicker every step along the street of the basket makers. People left their stalls to watch. But there was something in the rabbi's face that quieted them, dried up their curses. Nor did they beat him with the bottoms of their shoes. They stood with their shoes in their hands. But when the rest came through the crowd, they fell on them. They knocked the beams from their backs, tripped them, and kicked their private places, hurting them more because they'd let Jeshua of Nazareth go by.

Others in the crowd were kinder. The daughters of Jerusalem brought bowls of wine mixed with myrrh, which deadens pain. They held out their bowls and the men drank greedily. The rabbi didn't drink, I heard. By then the crowd had closed around us. I pushed through with Mary of Magdala, down through the vegetable market and the street of oil pressers, but the rabbi was already gone. We passed by minutes later, and though the streets were full, already nothing had happened on that hot morning. Already the people had forgotten, and the men were sitting in their stalls behind the piles of beans and melons. Men with empty faces argued with each other. Stupid women stood with baskets on their arms.

Golgotha was north of the Gennath gate. The road was full of gravel and white dust. It climbed through the poor houses and the broken walls, until it found an open space where four roads came together. Nearby, the gallows stood on a little hill. There were nineteen poles.

It was a place haunted by ghosts. Men and women had followed the prisoners through the gate, but now they turned away, drifted away. Mary of Magdala and I could see the men in front of us climbing the road, the wooden beams across their backs. We could see the soldiers, the decurion on horseback. Then we came out on Golgotha and there were no more houses, just flat shelves of the white rock. Among them piles of dung and then the smell of rotten meat, which came up suddenly and closed my throat. On one rock the Romans had laid out seven men from the week before. They had taken seven corpses from the gallows in the early morning, and laid them out. The corpses were black, covered with flies, and a boy kept watch. I couldn't look, and yet I saw each one.

Men were crucified on the sixth day of the week, their bodies left exposed over the sabbath. The Romans didn't let us take them down and bury them. Because of this, their souls had no graves to sleep in. North of the city near the village of Aceldama, there were tombs cut in the chalk cliffs. Many families were buried there, rich and poor. But these men the Romans killed were left out for the leopards and the dogs. At night their ghosts came to Golgotha and stood among the poles. No one passed there after dark, because of the armies of dead men. The way into the underworld is through the bottom of the grave.

That's where the steps lead down, the rocks cleave apart. But these men lay above the crossroads on the white rocks. There I stopped and couldn't go forward. The white dust covered my head, and I stood looking back toward the city. I listened to the buzzing of the flies. I looked back to the pinnacle of the temple under the bright sun, until Mary of Magdala took me by the sleeve.

She had not replaced her shawl. I was weeping, but in her face there was nothing like that, no womanly flaw. I looked into her eyes, the left one wandering. "Come," she said, and then she pulled me up the hill above the road, up onto Golgotha, the place of dry bones.

The soldiers kept us away from the gallows poles. But this is what we saw. The soldiers chose a man and laid him on his back down on the stones. They squatted over him and held his arms stretched out along the beam that he had carried from the city. Then the carpenter nailed him through the bones of his wrists and forearms while he screamed. The carpenter drove in four big, heavy-headed nails, and each nail required many strokes. Then they tied the man to the beam with ropes around his shoulders, so the nails wouldn't pull through his arms. They nailed down one man at a time, and the rest watched, huddled in a group.

A ladder stood against one of the poles, which were heavy and square, three times the height of a man. There was a slot across the pole below the top, where the beam fit in to make the cross. There was a smaller slot over the top of the pole.

Now I know every step it takes to crucify a man, because of that day. I watched it over and over again, fourteen times, and it took many hours to get them all up. This is how it was done. The man on the ladder had a thick rope which was made of two ropes twisted together. He slid the rope through the notch at the top of the pole, so it hung down on either side. The soldiers pulled the end of the rope down, and then pulled it apart into its two strands. They tied each strand around the beam, around the man's shoulders as he was nailed down. Then on the other side of the pole, the double rope was taken up by three prisoners. When the carpenter finished nailing the man to the beam and tying him down, the soldiers lifted up the beam by its two ends and carried it to the bottom of the pole. They carried it level with the man hanging down. Sometimes he struggled, and sometimes he hung senseless. The decurion raised his whip, and the three prisoners pulled on their end of the rope.

The soldiers pushed the ends of the beam over their heads. They let go, and the prisoners hoisted the beam up to the top of the pole until it fell into the slot, and the man on the ladder fastened it there, I don't know how. Sometimes it swung back and forth before he fastened it, because the man on the cross was kicking and screaming. But then the carpenter caught hold of his legs and tied them to the pole, above a small ledge in the wood, cut for the man to stand on. The carpenter had to climb on the ladder to tie his legs. All around there were flies on all the rocks.

The first man they crucified was Simon of Cyrene. He hung from the beam, senseless from the pain of nailing. The Romans wanted Jeshua of Nazareth to pull the rope, pull the crossbeam to the top of the gallows pole. The decurion had chosen Jeshua and two others, because they were the strongest. But though my lord was among criminals, he was not like them. He didn't take the rope the soldiers thrust into his hands. Though they beat him with their whips and the butts of their spears, he wouldn't take it. He struck out with his fist and a man fell. Then they were on him not just with their whips but with their knives. They cut him on his stomach and his buttocks and his head. I think one of them put out his left eye with the big knife, because I saw a red wound on his eye. The blood ran down his face, dripped from his chin.

I heard him shout. I heard his mother shouting too, cursing the Romans for their cowardice and damning them, cursing them with words I didn't know. She pushed through the soldiers and reached Jeshua where he lay. I think she touched him, but the decurion dragged her back. He slapped her, threw her down, kicked her away along the ground, and her cousin Salome crouched over her.

I watched this through my fingers. Mary of Magdala stood beside me, her face clean and calm. She made no movement. Her hair was around her shoulders.

I turned away from her and stepped a few paces away. The pain was worse when I crouched down, and so I stood to watch the two others hoist Simon to the top of the gallows. Though they were prisoners and knew they were to die, still they pulled on the rope with all their strength, eager in the work. In the end a soldier had to help them, and the three of them together pulled the beam into the slot, while the man on the ladder made the joint. Then he put a wooden marker at the top of the cross, with Simon of Cyrene's name in three languages.

Those two prisoners helped pull the rope for all the rest, and they were the last nailed up. That was their reward. That and the work, to take their minds away. They were young men, unmarked, unbruised. I wondered if they were Dimas and his brother Gestas, who fought the Romans in the temple. Later I walked through the poles, looking for their bodies, but I no longer recognized them. Only Simon's name was marked.

But now because of what the rabbi's mother had done, the soldiers pushed us back. We stood among some boulders. There were several women there and many children who had come up from the town. They weren't afraid. Mary of Magdala was on her knees, hiding her face sometimes and then looking up. I could see her lips move as she spoke some prayer, or talked to ghosts, or to herself.

The rabbi's mother stood near her cousin and would not be quiet. She shook her fists, shouting out curses while the tears ran down. "Sons of whores," she shouted. "Pig fuckers." And she threw stones and dirt not at the men on the crosses as the children did, but at the soldiers. Smiling, they raised their hands. But they did nothing, because she was an old woman.

With God's help the rabbi punished all of us. From the Antonia we heard the mid-day trumpets, which meant the sacrifices were to start. We heard the trumpets as they nailed him to the bar and crucified him on the outside circle of crosses. We moved around the hill to be most near him. We sat silent in the dry sand, the gravel and white dust. The sun was hot. There was no wind. The rabbi said nothing as the nails were put in. I thought he was already dead because he didn't move, his body was so torn.

After four hours, when the men were up, one of the soldiers passed among them with a long stick. At its top there was a sponge filled with poppy gum dissolved in vinegar. Something to ease the pain. Some men drank from it. But most didn't have the strength. They hung from their ropes and nails. Jeshua hung without moving, his head a mass of flies, and he didn't shake his head to drive them away.

After the fifth hour since Simon of Cyrene was crucified, the decurion sent soldiers to break the legs of the men who still cried out. The soldiers moved among the crosses with heavy sticks, and broke the men's legs above their ankles. In a few minutes they fell silent, because they couldn't breathe.

I stood up because I knew this was the end. In front of the soldiers with the sticks, another came with a long spear. One by one he stuck the men deep in their sides to see if they still lived. I thought he wouldn't raise a groan from Jeshua of Nazareth. Nor would my lord bleed from his wound, because he was already dead. But when the spear ran in under his ribs, my lord cried out. A stream of blood burst from his side. At that moment I felt the wind on my face, a big wind out of the desert that same moment, coming out of nothing. It rose around us in a whirlwind as Jeshua was crying out, and the hot dust blotted out the sun. The others scrambled to their feet, and we stood in the whirlwind with our hands over our heads. We couldn't see Jeshua of Nazareth. Around us rose a storm different from any I had seen before, or have seen now in forty years since. Different from any storm in Jerusalem, except God's anger which will come. A darkness came out of the bright day, a trembling in the earth. The rocks around us were thrown down. A crack opened in the ground under my foot, and the stones were sucked into it. Elsewhere houses split apart. Walls were shaken down. The sky was blotted out.

CHAPTER THREE:
THE OLD WOMAN

"It was evening, and I was laughing and crying as I went. I couldn't walk any farther, and my husband found a cave for me. He left me to find help from a house outside the walls. It was on the way to Bethlehem."

She has to say it was in Bethlehem. When she names this magic town, the young men nod. She can say anything as long as she says that: "I suffered with my second, but my first I barely felt under my heart. I sat in the cave's mouth and saw the birds stop in their flight. I saw a shepherd lift his stick, but he couldn't bring it down. I saw people eating in the fields. If they had bread in their mouths, they didn't chew. If they had cups, they didn't drink. But they were waiting. Their faces were turned toward the sky."

Or she says: "When I was alone in that cave, I could feel the world struggling as I struggled. There was a shaking in the ground. Leaves came down outside, and the branches of trees."

Or she says: "Once he was playing by the stream, and he drew water to make a fish pool. He made twelve sparrows out of mud and put them on the walls of the pool, three to each side. When he clapped his hands, the sparrows flew away, and Hanani's son fell into a fit. Later he knocked Jeshua down, pushed him in the street. And that boy was dead within a month."

Or she says: "In the land of Egypt a girl lay with a demon in the night. He came in through the window, and every morning she was a corpse sucked dry. Only she put one of the changing cloths around her neck. It was still wet with the child's piss, and it saved her. The smell protected her."

Or: "It was in a stable in Bethlehem. I thought he was ripping me apart. I lay bleeding in the straw, and he cried out. Kings sent by the prophet Zoradascht spoke to me when I was sleeping between the animals."

Sometimes she laughs when she tells the other women what she's said. Then Martha scolds her. "What a box of lies. Already Peter bar Jonah is making them drink his bath water and wash his feet."

Simon Bargiona is gone for good, she thinks. Peter bar Jonah has taken his place, even though his father's name was...what? Not Jonah, she's sure. Everyone knows it, or else used to. The old man is still alive someplace.

She sits by Jeshua's tomb in Bethany, or in the courtyard of the house when the weather's good. Serious young men come to visit her, to ask her questions. She's worried they might think her lazy, sitting there on the bench in the sun. She always tells them she was up before the light. Though now it's hard for her to pick things up and hold them, her fingers hurt so.

For the first years after her son's death she told them nothing. But the young men weren't discouraged. Now the stories come easily. They are harmless, she thinks, flowers on Jeshua's grave. She was alone in the world, and she did what she could for herself and her children. Sometimes it wasn't enough. Jeshua came to a bad end after all, which is something the young men forget. No one should see what she has seen.

Sometimes they bring money and she takes it. It's not the worst she's done. They wouldn't pay to hear how Joseph the carpenter threw her out in the cold weather. How she gave birth in a cold cave outside of Sepphoris in Galilee, a long way from Bethlehem. She might have died without her mother's help. Then there was a hard season of nothing before God sent Alpheus the Greek.

It was a long time ago. Though she's forgotten a good deal, some things she can never forget. Jeshua was her best child. If he was cruel sometimes, then she deserved it.

Now on the morning of the third day of the week comes Stephen of Antioch. He squats in the dust and talks in the Greek language. He's a beautiful young man with a straight nose. "So," she says, "is Bar Jonah as fat as ever?"

"He can hardly move. He sits on the table and no chair will hold him."

Could this be so? The young man smiles. "What does he eat?" she asks.

"No one can tell. He wears a mask over his face. Or else he goes by himself into the storage room, carrying a bucket."

The young man smiles, and she bursts out laughing.

"And when he shits, he fills up the entire hole," she says.

This one's more beautiful than the others. He's not so taken with Bargiona. And he's interested in her son. He'll ask what Jeshua said at such and such a place. If she doesn't know or can't remember, still she'll tell him something.

Jeshua told his students once, "Why trouble to listen, when you won't do what I say?" Now Bargiona and the nazorites had made her son into what they want, a mouthpiece for the Baptist, John. He used to rant about the coming darkness before Herod cut his head off.

"They'd let him eat the meat from their bones if he required it," Stephen says. "I'm joking, but that's how it is. He says they must share everything, which means he keeps it, he and a few others. The rest go hungry and thank him."

He's talking about Simon Peter. She laughs. "That's the way it always was."

Then: "Someone must complain," she says. "Some of the ones who knew my son."

"Thomas Didymus complains. So now they have a new story. They say when Jeshua the nazorite appeared to them, he still didn't believe."

She frowns. "What about Sicarius?" But the young man looks bewildered, and she has to explain: "Judas the zealot . . . "

"Oh, Ish Keriot. He doesn't live there anymore."

"Ish Keriot is not his name," she says. "Ish Keriot was someone else. Ish Keriot was Pilate's spy."

The young man shrugs. "He's very sick."

She's sitting on a bench in the courtyard under the sycamore tree. The wood is warm under her hands. "And you," she asks. "What about you? Have you found a way to tell the truth?"

In a moment all the beauty is gone out of his face, and he squints up at her. The sun has come out from behind a cloud. "God moves through human hands." He rubs his eye, pinches his ear. "I've seen Peter bar Jonah raise a cripple from his bed so that he walked for the first time."

"You told me that before. Now tell me about Sapphira and her husband."

He squats below her in the dust. His long hand is restless on his cheek, on the back of his neck. "Mother"—they often call her that. "What did you hear?"

She doesn't answer, but looks up. Above her the new leaves are coming. There are small birds among the branches. Stephen drops his forefinger into the dust and draws a circle.

"He was a rich man from Jericho," he says. "His name was Ananias. His wife had no sons, and they came to hear Peter speak. They came for three days, and Peter spoke with the power of the spirit, as he can. He took them to the desert where they saw the virgin of Magdala in her cave."

There are finches in the tree, moving down now from branch to branch.

"Ananias told us he would sell his land in Jericho and offer up the money. Peter's brother learned the price by chance, because he too was buying land. So when Ananias brought the money, Peter saw he'd kept some for himself."

"And?"

"God struck him dead. Andrew buried him where he couldn't be found."

"God must have wanted the money," Miriam says after a pause.

This makes Stephen angry. "Don't you see? He lied to us." Then he shakes his head. "Besides, he was already a sick man. A Roman citizen. How did he get so rich if not by stealing?"

Miriam says nothing for a while. Then—"Admit it. Say it. This could not have happened if my son had been alive."

They sit for a while in the hot air. Then Stephen looks up, his eyes wet. She smiles and puts her hand on his brown curls. She digs her crippled fingers into his hair.

"You should hear him when he speaks," he says of Simon Peter. "God gives him strength."

She laughs. "I've known him since he was a child."

She's astonished she can touch this boy and he doesn't flinch away. Maybe she can do anything here in this courtyard, in this house. Outside the gate the world is as it was. But here, Martha and Mary have made a place to live.

The two sisters are with the day workers. Sarah the Egyptian is inside with the sick woman. The hot weather has come, and it makes the air heavy and quiet in the afternoon. Miriam's thoughts are sluggish too. Still it astonishes her that she can sit with her face uncovered, her hand on Stephen's hair, protected by the house, her age, the innocence of these men who follow her son.

"I've heard there are women with you," she says. "Have you thought about a wife?"

He frowns and shakes his head. She lifts her hand away. He looks toward the open gate. "There's no time."

He's impatient, she can tell. Why talk of marriage to a man who's counting every sunset and dead locust? She does it to tease him, which he knows.

Still it makes her sad how much they've forgotten in a few years. Her son never spoke of the last days. Why should poor men fight against the rich at the world's end? Why should they work to love each other, to forgive?

But still the boy is beautiful, sulking now, his lips and forehead. His brown curls. She closes her aching hand above his head, returns it to her lap.

She wants to go inside the house to see if anything has changed. To see if the woman is still crying, because it was her crying that drove

Miriam out into the courtyard in the hot day. She couldn't stand that noise. "Come," she says to tease the boy, make him smile, chase him away. "Let me tell you something."

Lately all her stories have been about the land of Egypt. She might have gone that far if she could have managed it, alone and penniless and with a child. She might have gone and not come back. Women own houses in Egypt, money, animals. That's what Sarah says, who's Martha's slave. They marry for love, even each other, for comfort's sake.

She knows nothing about the land of Egypt, except what Sarah tells them. But she says, "It took us forty days to cross from Gaza. We went through the desert mountains, my husband and I and the young child. King Herod would have killed us, so we walked by night and rested in the heat of the day. At first the land was parched and barren, full of broken rock. But then we came into the river valley, the greenest place in God's world, where no one is hungry. There are no beggars, whores, or bandits on the road.

"But there is a spirit called Set who lives in the statues. He comes out of the temples in the middle of the towns. All roads lead to him. The statue comes alive, and walks into the town in the shape of a boy. Where we were staying, he came through the door and touched the face of our host. He was an old man with a young wife, and that night was his first with her, because they were just married. But the spirit reached into his clothes and grabbed his balls, so he couldn't give her pleasure, that night or seven nights afterward, which is how long we stayed in that town. All day he would be stiff and hard as a club, but at night when he went in, he would shrivel up to nothing when she touched him.

"On the seventh morning the woman came to me where I sat with my child nursing. She asked me for a medicine, a charm to say. I told her to touch my son, take him in her arms. So she lifted him up, and he woke and began to cry. He was the age of his first tears, and I told her to rub his tears onto her fingers. The medicine was not for her but for her husband. If she rubbed herself and the old man—no, I'm teasing you."

She's succeeded. Stephen's on his feet, blushing and confused—"Mother, please don't laugh. I know you're angry for Sapphira's sake."

"Yes," she says. "Now go away."

It's true. As she looks into his startled face, she feels her anger rise. "You lump of shit," she says. "You don't come back." She spits into the dust.

All the time she spends with men, especially these followers of her dead son, her anger isn't far away. But a strange part of getting old, she thinks as she watches Stephen of Antioch back away from her, is how she can no longer understand her feelings. Sometimes her laughter comes up out of nothing. Sometimes at night she can feel her heart pounding and her fear come up. Now suddenly she's in a rage—what for? When he was talking about Sapphira's husband, she'd felt nothing but sensations of the body, a prickling on the skin of her hands.

Now the prickling comes back as her rage subsides. Now suddenly the young man seems beautiful again, and she's sorry for his look of hurt disgust. When he's gone, she sits for a few minutes thinking about her son. She can't remember punishing him when he was young, though he was not obedient. Jeshua's brother Jacob, she used to have to beat him.

God must have wanted the money, she thinks. She's sitting in the yard at Bethany with the red dust between her toes. Finches quarrel above her in the sycamore tree, and she listens as she tries to move her cramped fingers.

When the anger is gone, a sadness comes. It stays with her as she goes in. She pokes aside the blanket in the doorway. The air in the big room is stuffy and cool.

A clay lamp burns on the table, a small flame, disturbed once as she lets the blanket fall. Her eyes adjust, her hearing too. Or else now she is searching for the sound, a whimper from the inner room. Not Lazarus's room, but on the other side where her son used to stay, when he was a guest in Simon the leper's house. For a moment the image of her son comes back to her, and she sees him as he stood in that same doorway once in the year before his death. His big hands and shoulders, his dark face invisible. But then the whimpering distracts her, and she rubs her mouth. Whatever happens or has happened, this woman doesn't please her. This woman has been crying and wailing as if the sadness in the world belonged to her. Yet Miriam watched her own son tied to a tree. She held his dead body after he was cut down, and she never shed a tear.

Besides, no one but a fool would give money to Simon Peter Bargiona. However else the story went, Sapphira's husband sold some land and paid the money to those thieves while she stood by. If God struck Ananias down, perhaps it was to punish him for stupidness. Who knows? Sometimes thieves and murderers do God's will. God struck Simon the leper too, whose house this was. God struck him on the night of her son's death, killed him for his faults, and so he wouldn't turn her son away from Lazarus's tomb.

Now she sees Martha standing at the inside doorway, stretching out her solid arm. She sees the gleam of gold around Martha's neck under the ragged line of her short hair.

The gleam of the chain reminds Miriam of Nazareth she's a guest in this house. Every day, she's a guest. She no longer thinks about Martha's dyed dress and soft shirt, the silver belt around her waist. But she hates the chain and always looks for it. At the same time, her tongue searches her back teeth.

She stares at the woman, but can't understand the words she's mouthing. So Miriam crosses the dark room and follows her through the inside curtain. She stoops under the door frame. Sapphira of Jericho lies on the bed, weeping to herself.

Martha gestures toward some pillows on the floor near the lamp, which stands on a footstool in a corner of the room. She puts her arm out to help, but there's nothing wrong with Miriam's knees. She sits on the carpet, which covers part of the dirt floor.

Martha sits down too. "She's told me everything."

Now Sarah the Egyptian comes in from the store room with a jar of oil in her hand. She squats over the bed, and with a wet cloth she washes the bruises on the woman's face and neck, the places on her scalp where the hair has been torn away. Sapphira cries out, and cries even more when the Egyptian puts her hands under her clothes.

Jeshua could have cured her, the old woman thinks. He was skillful in that way. Then she listens to Martha. "It was Andrew and Philip. Bargiona sent them: they're the worst of them. They were looking for the money her husband gave her for the temple, but she's hidden it. They stole her rings and bracelets."

"It must have been a lot of money."

"It was a lot of money. Do you think they would have taken this trouble for a few sesterces? There's a risk involved. Her husband was a citizen. He knew the magistrate."

A sadness comes over Miriam as she sits. Her tongue searches for the ache in her back tooth. "He owned seven houses in Jericho," Martha continues. "A field of fruit trees near the river. That's what she says, but it's probably more. Her husband sold three houses and gave the money to Simon Peter. He never said he'd sell it all."

Miriam is watching Sarah the Egyptian as she squats over the woman's head. Miriam watches Sarah's long hands as she mixes honey into the oil. She watches her earrings and dark, corded neck. Her hair is bound up in a rag.

"Her husband was vomiting blood every morning," Martha says. "He was an old man. Peter said he could cure him."

Miriam swallows some of the spit that is in her mouth. Then she finds her voice. "If this woman knows the magistrate, maybe she should say something to him. Maybe I should. The soldiers are still interested in Simon Bargiona. That's why he's changed his name."

The Egyptian's hands stop moving over the woman's dress. "You'd do that?" says Martha.

Miriam spits into the corner of the room. "Tell me what happened."

The Egyptian pulls Sapphira over onto her side. Now for the first time Miriam sees her face. Coated now with oil, it shines in the lamp light. There's a crust of blood in her nostrils and around her lips. Her eyes are swollen shut. Miriam is surprised she's so young.

Martha shrugs. "They went to see the madwoman in the cave. Ananias was frightened, and promised to pay all his money for a cure. Later he sold three houses and gave a thousand pieces of silver to those thieves. Seven hundred, he put aside to offer at the temple for his guilt. She knows where it's hidden. She wants to keep it, because her husband's dead. His brother has already taken the rest of the property. She doesn't want to be a servant in his house."

Miriam has no patience for these stories about money. "She should have had a son," she grumbles, confused by her own harshness.

"And if her husband was too old, she should have taken a son from the Greek towns," she continues, watching the Egyptian's hands as she pauses once again to listen. She's pushed Sapphira onto her stomach and is touching her naked back.

Martha laughs, a grunting, nervous sound. "Old woman, what are you saying? You want to give Bar Jonah to the Romans. Then you're scolding this girl as she lies here with a broken nose. But I remember when my father died, you saved my life."

When God struck Simon the leper down, his cousins came to take his money. But they listened to Miriam for the sake of her son, who'd raised Lazarus from death. Miriam led them to the room where Lazarus lay. So the men left the house and half the land until Lazarus should die again, which they expected every month. They took the money, the stored grain, the animals. The women, they allowed to stay. No one wanted to take them in.

"Whatever I did, you repaid me," Miriam says.

"Maybe this woman will repay you too."

Miriam of Nazareth holds up her hands. The pain in them is hard to bear. They always hurt, the right more than the left. Sometimes she feels a burning deep in the small bones. Then they go numb, and she can barely feel her fingers when she's moving them. Her knuckles are swollen. The skin on her palms feels thin, worn away. The backs of her hands are covered with red spots.

She used to chew her nails, but now they've all grown in. Sometimes she looks at her hands and thinks they must belong to another woman. She can't be sure, but she thinks she might once have had fingers like the Egyptian's—strong and thin. She imagines the yarn she's twisted in her life might fill the house. She used to get up before dawn to wash the piles of clothes and beat them on the rocks and twist them dry, and then go working in the barley, picking stones, always for other people.

Now she says to Martha, "Don't laugh. Don't you remember?"

Simon the leper used to beat his daughters, Martha especially. He'd lain with her after her mother died—a common story. No, but a sad one. These things change a woman, not for the better. Was Miriam the only one who thought there'd been a child? Now she remembers Martha the night of her father's death, rocking back and forth, exhausted, in tears.

"I'm your slave here," Miriam says, "no matter how old I get. I'll do what you tell me."

Now again there are tears in Martha's eyes. What's wrong with these women? Miriam thinks. They cry over nothing, a few hard words.

"We don't keep you," Martha says.

"Where would I go?" Jeshua is dead. Jacob is with the synagogue. The rest are in Galilee. They have children of their own. "I'll stay with the body of my son," she says. "Those bastards might steal it from the tomb."

Now the old woman's anger is gone suddenly. It's just that she gets tired. She reaches out with her right hand and puts it on Martha's cheek, her hair. Though she hardly knows what she's doing, what she's touching—her hand's a block of wood. "Shut your mouth," she says. "Don't listen to me."

And just as quickly she has to swallow to keep her laughter down. She puts both hands on Martha's neck, and then around her shoulders. She embraces her, putting her cheek against Martha's cheek, squinting down at the gold necklace until she closes her eyes. She feels the laughter coming—what for? There is nothing to laugh about. But she whispers in Martha's ear so the Egyptian won't hear. "The money belongs to me," she says. "Ananias promised it to me. I'll go squeeze it out of Simon Bargiona, and I'll buy back the wheat field you had to sell."

It's the truth, though now Martha pulls away, is looking at her as if she were crazy. But Ananias came four times to see her in the courtyard. That was how his wife knew the house, so she could find refuge here.

Four times Ananias had come and squatted in the dust of the courtyard. Miriam told him stories, and he knelt to kiss her hands, though he was a rich old man. When she said how poor she was, he'd promised to help. Now she thinks someone must have overheard.

She is staring at the Egyptian's hands. "Have you searched her?" she says. "Maybe she is carrying a piece of paper. Seven hundred drachmae is a lot of money."

But Martha has grabbed hold of her hand. "What are you talking about?"

The air is dark and stuffy in the little room. It stinks of scented oil. She's watching the Egyptian's fingers, watching them pause again. "Let me go. Bargiona will listen to me, or else give me something. I'm talking about seven hundred drachmae at least."

"Hush, be quiet. They are dangerous men."

"Is that what you think? I've known them since they were children."

Martha is trying to soothe her, hold onto her wrist, but she twists her hand away, angry now, and for good reason. Jeshua was her son. She bore him and made him strong. When he was dead, she stole his body from the Romans, carried it to this place. That is what strength is, to get back what is yours. And what is money anyway but a lump of shit, as her son often said.

Praise God Miriam's legs are strong, and she can walk if she has to. She's taller than these women. When she stands up she has to stoop under the ceiling. "I'll be back before dark," she says. "But I won't go without food. Some roots in lamb broth—my teeth are good."

But there's always the little ache, and her tongue finds it now.

* * *

Later she agrees to take the younger girl, her namesake, Simon the leper's younger daughter. "Don't you trust me?" she says. In fact she's glad, because the girl soothes her. She's not like her sister or the black Egyptian. She's a small thing, sweet-skinned, with dark eyebrows and soft eyes. She's six years past the marrying time, and she will never marry. There's no dowry, and her father is dead. There's a confusion in her family, which men and their mothers hate. And of course that matter of Cleopas, whose thumb left a dirty mark.

She spends her days in the kitchen garden or at the grinding stone, or washing and feeding her brother Lazarus, who never rises from his bed. She doesn't complain. It's a comfortable house. But sometimes there's a sorrow that surrounds her. Miriam sees it because the girl loves her, not just for her son's sake. The girl watches her, listens to her, believes her, not like the others. But too much patience is as bad as none. Sometimes Miriam sits muttering stories. Sometimes she curses and grumbles as the girl stands in front of her, listening with the eyes of a calf. Then suddenly Miriam wants to reach up and pinch her nose and cheek, punish her for indulging an old woman, making her feel older still.

Now this afternoon the girl walks behind her, carrying a basket of onions from the cellar. But as they pass Gesthemene, Miriam pauses to let her catch up. She wants to talk to her, tell a few jokes to calm her nervousness, because what Martha said was true. Andrew and Philip and the rest are dangerous men. To some men she can say, "Jeshua of Nazareth was my son," and they will listen. These students of his are not among them.

Now she stands beside the wall, waiting for the girl to catch up. The hot weather has come, and there's no water in the ditch. "In the land of Egypt," Miriam says, "it was nothing like this. The hills were green even in summer."

The girl looks up at her. She must know where Miriam has spent her life. But she pauses and looks around. They are in the place where Jeshua was taken by the Romans.

"In the land of Egypt," Miriam says, "everything was strange until my son was there. People slept all day and worked all night. They lived in the stables and put their donkeys in the houses. Chickens and ducks spoke in the synagogue. Horses swam in the river, and fish walked on dry land."

This is where her son was taken, by this corner of the wall. Miriam often stops here. "When it rained or snowed, they slept outside," she says, closing her eyes. "Women plowed the fields while the men made bread. Romans were slaves with chains around their wrists. Monkeys wore clothes and rode on horseback."

When she opens her eyes, she sees the tears on the girl's face. What's wrong with her? she thinks, fierce now. "Men beat their wives and loved their enemies."

"Tell me a story about your son," the girl says.

And so they go on again, down into Kidron and under the city wall. The story Miriam tells is as true as she can make it after all these years: Once when Jeshua was a little boy, he and some others were throwing rocks into a tree. A crow fell, stunned. When some of the boys rushed toward it with sticks in their hands, Jeshua drove them away. He bit

Hanani's son. He came home covered with dust and the bird in his hands, pecking at his hands till the blood came. It had a broken wing. It never flew again, but he took care of it. He fed it with his fingers, and it lived for several years outside the house.

When they come to the Fountain gate, they put on their veils, although the heat is stifling. Miriam can't see the stones in front of her. She's forever stumbling and grunting, knocking her old toes. But the girl walks gracefully, carrying the basket on her head.

Miriam imagines there might be soldiers at the gate and in the streets, because of the rumors about Caesar's statue. She sees no one. Maybe they're at the temple. She's heard the garrison's been reinforced.

But this is not the place for soldiers. There are no streets in this part of the lower town. This was the area that burned after the Romans killed her son. It was never rebuilt, but rather grew up little by little in clusters of mud houses filled with animals and men. The houses are divided by ditches of wet mud. Dogs and chickens struggle through them looking for water and food. There's not a village in Galilee that smells as bad in the hot weather.

Ragged children play in the dirt. Men sit drinking in the shade. This is where thieves and bandits live, the friends who led Jeshua to death.

They come to a low door. Men sit in a line to the right side of it. She tries to push in past the ragged blanket, but one of the men stands up to challenge her, a gap-toothed, cross-eyed fool. He tries to grab her by the wrist. "Animal," says Miriam of Nazareth. She reaches out to slap him with her other hand, but he's too quick. Now he's got her by both wrists, laughing through his broken teeth. She tries to kick him but he jumps away. Other men are rising now. Some have sticks in their hands. Would they beat an old woman? "Pigs," she calls them, and they pause. Then one of them grabs her veil and pulls it back.

They've knocked the girl's basket from her head, and one of them is picking up the onions. He's so stupid, he's stealing a gift, thinks Miriam, blinking in the sudden light. Her old eyes fill with tears. She's staring at the man's hands. The nails on both his thumbs are black and loose.

Then his hands stop moving and she's looking at his face. His nose is big. His ears stick out from his head. He's dropped the onions and is squatting on his heels, a stupid look on his face.

Bargiona has been praising her today, she thinks. Or else the lies she tells have been repeated here, sharpened by dull tongues. Some men are on their knees now, staring as if they hoped to hear God's words in her mouth—"You penis-sucking pigs," she says, "what are you doing?"

They never looked at her son this way, not even when he raised Lazarus. It makes her angry. None of these bastards would walk an hour to comfort an old woman as she sits in her yard at Bethany. Not that she'd let them in the gate.

"Pick those up," she says, and two of them are scrabbling for the onions in the dirt. Tears are in her eyes, which makes her angry. The night she cut her son down from the tree, she had no tears. But maybe she's a weak woman after all, ready for the tomb.

She pulls the veil from her head to show her gray hair. One of the men is on his hands and knees in front of her. She takes a step, lifts her foot to kick him in the side, but pauses. These men are ridiculous the way they stare at her, their faces like scared goats, and the girl too. Miriam wants to paint their faces with her spit. She wants to squat and piss on the threshold of their house. Who's she? A poor woman from the streets of Sepphoris. Her father was a deaf mute. At thirteen she lay down for a Roman soldier and started all this.

The laughter that sprays out of her is high and forced. And it brings a small relief, a small vision of Pantherus the Syrian, to whom she gave herself so freely that spring when the twelfth legion was in Sepphoris. Long ago when she was young. Once she had him in the forest against the trunk of a locust tree. He was a brown-haired Goliath, bigger than any Jew.

But it's a sad joke that leads her from that time to this. Jeshua on the tree. Sapphira in the house at Bethany. Women are the stem of evil as the rabbis say, the fountain of bad luck.

Now she sees Thaddeus in the doorway. He's dressed in a white shirt. His hands and face are clean. He's a handsome, sharp-eyed, smiling brute. He holds aside the blanket and beckons her in from the hot sun. What's wrong with her? Her voice and breathing are unsteady.

Her heart knocks. Yet she came here to go in, to grab Simon Peter by the beard and wag his fat head from side to side. Oh Jeshua, my son.

Eyes blind, she finds herself in a small room. She has to stoop under the ceiling, though both Thaddeus and the girl behind her stand erect. When the blanket falls, the only light comes through moth-eaten holes. She can't breathe in here. It's a place for rats, but Thaddeus beckons her forward and she follows through an inner door and then a maze of hot, black, stinking, airless rooms, all empty, she thinks, though she can't see. Thaddeus has a lamp now and she follows it, stooping so as not to bump her head. It's a house built for animals and dwarves.

Now the rooms are bigger. Shadows move beside her. She comes out into a large courtyard which is partly open to the sky. And there he is, Simon Peter Bargiona, surrounded by men who have come out of the desert to follow him, fooled by his stories and the madwoman of Magdala.

Miriam stands blinking in the crowd, for the courtyard is full. Bargiona hasn't seen her yet. He sits under a canopy in a wooden chair, talking to some men standing behind him. As she watches, one points to her, his arm outstretched.

She's surprised by the number of people who surround her, a hundred, maybe more. She never saw Jeshua preach to more than twenty. These others who sit waiting in the bright sun, no more than a handful ever knew him. The rest are woman-hating nazorites or "watchers," followers of the Baptist from the desert villages, keepers of the law, counting the minutes till the world's end.

When Jeshua was alive, not one would have crossed the street to listen. Now they flock to him and call him the hope of all the Essene prophecies—a pierced man rising from the dead. They think each part of Jeshua's life contains a sign for them. Nor do they remember what he said. But they argue whether God forced a likeness between two words, Nazareth and nazorite, which is what they've called themselves for a hundred years.

There's a stench that comes out of the scrawny bodies of these men. One stands in front of her, his thin shoulders shaking with prayer. She feels a gust of laughter—these men, she thinks, no wonder they are full of hate. What woman would go with them out of choice? No, but their mothers, sisters, wives, and daughters touch themselves under their clothes. Then they find soldiers to lie with in the ditches and beside the roads. Anyone as long as he's uncircumcised. How else could they earn money of their own? How else could they find joy? Not with these boys, praying for the world's end. Even to look at a woman's body is against their law.

She stands blinking in the light, her shawl around her neck. Grinning suddenly, she wonders how she came to such an evil mind. When she was young she never thought about such things.

But there are many kinds of people in the yard. She comes to see them grudgingly, not just watery young men, but children, girls, and women more decrepit even than she, waiting in the sun. On the dais, under a canvas canopy, dressed in white, are Jeshua's friends. She saw them with him many times, and now her heart warms with pain and gladness. She can almost believe he's still alive as she looks from face to bearded face.

Bargiona's a small man, and he'll always be small, she thinks, no matter how much he eats. Now he is standing beside his chair, and to tell the truth he's less fat than she'd imagined. His arms and legs are thin. He has no neck. His bald head sits between his shoulders, and his beard hangs down his chest. His belly hangs over his belt. He's got a rich man's stomach.

He's talking. But the noise out of the crowd makes it hard to hear. She takes a few steps forward, and people stand aside to let her pass. She puts her hand up to her ear, angry at herself, because her hearing has gone weak this spring, especially in crowds.

Muttering curses under her breath, she takes a few steps more. She strains to listen to the well-remembered voice, but what she's hearing make no sense in Greek or any of the tongues of Galilee. After a minute she takes down her hand. When she first met Simon Bargiona, he was a fisherman on Gennesaret. She'd bet a drachma he never learned to read his name.

Now she starts to laugh. Nothing she's heard could mean anything in any language. Bargiona is grunting and howling like a beast. "Shoo, shoo, shoor," he sings, each word stupider than the last, yet everyone is listening. She feels a new small admiration, because of the plainness of the trick.

Jacob is beside him on the dais now. Of all her children he is the most like Jeshua in the lines of his face. Pantherus gave Jeshua his size and power, but the faces of her oldest children came from her, as everyone said. So it hurts her to see Jeshua's head on that weak frame, those narrow shoulders, those small thighs. Jacob's head has always seemed too heavy for his strength.

She's scarcely spoken to him since he abandoned his own brother to the soldiers and threw himself in with Bargiona and the rest. Now she wonders what he's thinking—he was a stubborn child. He envied Jeshua but loved him too, and she wonders what he makes of this. A space has opened in front of the dais, and a lot of sick people have come into it. There's a whole line of them in front of Bargiona, and he comes down from his chair to put his hands on their heads, singing in his made-up language. His tongue flickers in his mouth.

"La lila lilalu," he says. And now Miriam no longer hears him in the noise of the crowd, no longer sees him in the press. Instead she shifts her feet in the red dust and wonders where the girl has gone. Surely she followed her. Surely she didn't stay with Thaddeus in the dark.

There's a space around her where the people have pulled away. She looks down to see the dust on her shins and the hem of her dress—she'll ask Sarah to wash it. Jacob sees her now, stares toward her with a grim expression, and she feels a sadness, a prickling in her hands. He was strict in all the laws when he was young. He used to argue with his brother—Miriam knows nothing about such things. Because she is a woman. But there are laws against trickery and deceit.

Jeshua was always skillful with his hands. She'd taught him her remedies, and he'd learned more when he was working in the market at Sepphoris. There'd been a Greek when he went east, walking the world's roads—a Greek that taught him. He cured many with his herbs and poultices as he wandered through Israel and across the lake. He had a skill for setting bones—people still spoke of it. But he'd not slapped them on their heads as Bargiona did. Jeshua never shook them by the shoulders, muttering foolish charms. He knew the same cure wasn't good for everything.

The sun shines on the white mud walls of the courtyard. A roaring noise, a hammering light seems to fill the yard, and she feels faint. God, my God, she thinks for no reason. She bows her head. She feels the sun hammer down on her bare head, and so she covers it with her shawl. She can't lift her head to see the men on the dais, nor does she see Philip of Bethsaida take the serpents from their basket. It's a round basket underneath his chair, and he stoops to bring them out. Sluggish from the dark, they weave and strike, and the people fall back. He holds them in his hands. They are ringed with colors and they open their sharp jaws, but they won't hurt him. They curl around his forearms and he holds them up.

Later she'll say she remembers the false healing and false words, the sickness in her stomach and the weakness in her head. But she was there a long time. Later she won't admit to coming forward when Bargiona speaks her name. But she'll remember it. He called her name, and she walked to him like a whore, she'll think. But she'll be lying to herself, because at that moment she feels his strength and the people's fear. A wind blows through the courtyard, and she feels it. The men and women sink down to their knees, or they are prostrate in the dust. Men on crutches hobble forward. Lepers with their swollen arms. Later she'll deny the truth. But even as she spits out words of her contempt, she'll keep inside of her the memory of Peter bar Jonah, his face shining with a light. The sweat pours from his face. There's a noise in her ears like the ringing of a bell. She stumbles forward, and beside her crawls a boy with a twisted spine, dragging his legs like a broken spider. Of her own will she goes down on her knees. Nor did she speak to him about Sapphira's husband or the money. Nor did she slap his cheeks. Instead she let him bend down and embrace her, raise her up onto the dais and call her the mother of the one Christ. When she turned around, everyone was holding out their hands. Tears came to her eyes, and then she was moving through the crowd while men and women touched her hands. If there were any sick people, she laid her hands on them, because she thought, Why not? What harm can it do? These are the people who loved Jeshua, my son.

She never talks to Simon Peter, who disappears into the house. As the crowd is dispersing, Jacob comes. "Mother," he says, but she turns away. Instead she takes the hands of Thomas Didymus, a slow, shy, ugly man whose brows join over his thick nose. He stayed with Jeshua until the end. He whispers in her ear: "Where are you going now? Have you eaten? May I come see you at your house?"

But as he's talking she remembers Mary of Bethany, who is not there. Thomas Didymus is squeezing her hands, hurting them, and she pulls away. Dazed and smiling, she stoops under the lintel again and into the dark, crowded rooms. "Help me find her," she says. "You know Lazarus's sister who came with me."

"Judas Sicarius sends his greeting," Didymus says. And then more but she doesn't listen. She retraces her steps, full of apprehension. She's right: men sit in the darkness, gathered around a lamp. They grin at her, touching their oiled beards. They have knives in their belts. But she isn't afraid of these bastards. Hands aching, she steps past them, pushes through the curtain in the doorway. "Mary," she says. In the hot darkness of the inner room, Thaddeus has the girl by her long hair.

She doesn't need Thomas Didymus, she thinks. "Pig," she says, coming forward. The air is thick as broth. Thomas Didymus grabs the bastard and is slapping him, while she puts her arms around the girl.

There's no reason to talk. "Come," she says, and they go out, while Thomas pushes the man down against the bags of grain. He's not fighting back; he's laughing while the older man slaps him. She curses at the ones sitting outside. None of them has moved.

Later she curses her own weakness as she walks along the road. She's just a stupid woman after all, she thinks, striding forward through the dust. The girl limps behind her out of breath. She is carrying the empty basket, her veil tied three times around her face. How can she breathe? Miriam is full of anger. Both of them were handled by these men.

But now she hears the sound of running footsteps, and she turns. It is Didymus again, and a boy she recognizes. He keeps a stall in the Xystus where he sells Judas Sicarius's pots.

They are carrying sticks, and the girl raises her hands. But no, they want to protect them. "You filthy pigs," mutters Miriam, too tired to yell.

The road curves around the bottom of the hill of Olives. Didymus follows them until they stop at the juncture. Then he approaches. "Are you hurt?" he says to the old woman. He is too ashamed even to look at the girl.

"You disgust me," Miriam answers, because she disgusts herself.

"These are terrible times," Didymus says, and Miriam turns aside to spit into the dust. "I will come see you in your house—not now," he says. The boy comes forward holding a small blue pot, which he has taken from his bag.

"It's a present from my master," he says. He bows his head.

She can't bring herself to break it in the dust. She pokes her finger into it, but there is nothing inside. "You see," she says. She motions with her chin. "There's the well. We're almost home."

But she won't go any farther until Didymus turns back. He looks over his shoulder several times, and then he is out of sight around a turning of the road. Miriam stands rubbing at the pot with her shawl. The glaze is as blue as Lake Tiberias in Galilee. There is no place where it is cracked. Then she thrusts the pot into the breast of her dress.

Bethany is on her right hand among the hemp fields, the first houses and the well. To her left the road continues through a steep defile toward Jericho and the salt lake. She looks at the shadows of the trees, the lump of her own shadow on the rocks. The heat of the day is past. But they can't reach the cave and then return before dark. It's too far.

She goes down to the well at the bottom of a hollow near the road. There's water in the stone trough. She uncovers her head to wash her face and drinks for a long time, filling her gut. Three veiled women take their pots and turn away—they never speak to her. They hate her in this town, because she is from Galilee.

The girl watches, puzzled. Then she shrugs her shoulders and unwraps her shawl, and Miriam sees she has been weeping. Her face is flushed, her eyes are smudged with tears. Miriam wets the sleeve of her dress. "We won't go back tonight," she says. The girl won't answer, but stands without flinching as Miriam scrubs her face, her hands too old and clumsy to be gentle.

"Please, " she says. "I want to go home."

A cloud of flies buzzes around them. Miriam shakes her head. She has no wish to admit what she's done, how she left the girl alone, how she put her hands on Bargiona's head and blessed him. She can't say it, not with that woman lying bruised and beaten on the couch and the Egyptian standing over her. No, it will be better to spend some nights out of doors without water in the rocks—a good lesson for both of them. The news of what they've done is following them, she's sure. But she doesn't want to speak the words and shame herself for nothing. If she comes back and the story is already there, then no one will speak of it. She can curse and be silent.

There was a time when she could work all day in the sun without a drink. She didn't sleep under a roof for years together. In Nazareth she had a corner of the dusty yard when she was a servant for the old man. He used to poke her with a stick to wake her. But then he died and she would squat to piss on his grave whenever she went by it. She had been harder then.

So she walks over the crust of dry red mud, through the ring of cut stones and up to the road again. "You can go back if you want," she says. "I'm going to see my daughter-in-law." She turns her back on the village of Bethany. The girl has to hurry to catch up.

They walk for hours with the red sun behind them. The road moves back and forth between the rocks, and in some places the defile has been cut, because this is an old place. Armies have marched here, and the pilgrims of the east. Under their boots and the hooves of their animals, the boulders have been broken to a sharp gravel that hurts Miriam's feet. But she strides onward and the girl limps behind her past the ruins of the sentinel tower, into the dry wilderness. The land changes as if God had drawn the border between Benjamin and Judah. And though she knows that each step brings her lower, deeper toward the lake and the dry plain, still it seems to Miriam as if she's always scrambling uphill. She sees no one, even though this is where bandits live, Samaritans and Arabs in the rocks above the road. But maybe they see nothing to tempt them in an old woman, a girl with her empty basket. Or maybe now the wind has come up and the air is full of grit, they have abandoned their places and gone home to Sichem or their black tents in the desert, for she sees no one, not even a bird.

For hours they climb through the sharp boulders beside the road, keeping out of sight as best they can. On either side she can see ridge after ridge of yellow and brown rock. She is looking for the trail, and then in front of her she sees the red cliff of the Blood Ascent which marks the border. The haze from the red sun glows around them.

They rest for a moment before they climb up from the road. At one time this was a bandit's trail marked by secret stones. But now many pilgrims come this way, and she can see their footprints in the dust. Sharp clefts, filled now with shadow, open up beside the trail. In the twilight the landscape comes alive, and sometimes it appears to her not as a wilderness of shattered stone, but as the ruins of a city greater than Jerusalem. It's a fancy that takes hold of her moment by moment as she tires, and the dead, meaningless rocks rise up, inhabited by ghosts. Now suddenly a brittle ridge becomes a line of broken pillars, and all around her she can see the walls of broken palaces where dead giants lived, the sons of Asmodeus, maybe, whose towers were crushed by God.

The walls of Jerusalem are scarcely out of sight. In winter it rains every week, here not a drop. What's the reason, except God's curse? Jeshua would have laughed at her for such a thought, and of course he was right and she is wrong, a fanciful old fool. Still it's hard not to be frightened as darkness falls.

When Jeshua was young she used to tell him all about the flood, the fiery bush, the man and woman in the garden. He'd laugh and she'd laugh too. As he got older, he refused to listen. He was interested in men, not ghosts. Justice, not magic, he told her once. But at the end he was as bad as Peter Bargiona with his sorcery. Why had he plucked Lazarus from death? Why had he put his curse on Simon the leper, who lay in the dirt of his own store room without a mark? Was it because he needed a dead dog to greet him at the gates of Sheol? No—she understood. It was to make a refuge for his old mother, a safe place for himself.

She sits down on a rock to rub her feet and wait. She's tired and old and out of breath, but still she's harder than these girls who'd sleep all day if someone didn't wake them. Minutes pass. On the slope above her, a jackal stands on a rock above a broken slope. The wind is cold now, and she wraps her shawl around her shoulders.

The girl stands in front of her. "Please," she says. "I can't go on."

"It's not far now."

"Please, I'm so thirsty, and my feet are bleeding. Let me rest."

"It's not far. We want to get there before dark."

She has no idea how far it is. She's never been here. She's scarcely seen the mad woman, Jeshua's widow, since the week of his death, and she only knows the way because Stephen of Antioch described it. There's less dust on the rocks here, and it's been a long time since she's seen footprints.

But how could they be lost? The trail lies in front of her. It climbs between two hills of stone whose flanks are smoothed and healed now in the silver light. A pregnant moon shines over the mountains in the east, protectress of women, gaining strength in the black sky now that the sun has set. From it a new light fills the valley. She raises her arm and feels the wet glow on her hand, cleaning the burns of day.

She looks up the western slope again. The jackal is gone. And it's not just a trick of fear, but she's staring at the white cube of rock where it was standing. In the new light she can see it's been shaped. The corners are too fine. Closer to hand lies a flat piece of stone, and she can see a crude pattern of leaves carved along one edge.

"Look," she says.

Above them stands a gate of two raised stones, though the lintel has fallen. Miriam climbs toward it and the girl follows, still complaining. But soon she's out of breath again, or too far back to hear. Miriam climbs upward by herself, and under her feet the path is wider, more distinct, the stones clean and secure. In some places a stair has been cut into the rock.

She passes through the cleft, and on the other side the slope drops gently away. Below her she sees bushes and even some small trees. As she descends, the rock turns into sand and dust, and she finds herself in a small valley. She smells water and then sees it, a silver pool under the moon. She sees the tents of pilgrims camped under the rocks, and among them here and there the flicker of small fires. Columns of smoke rise to the windless air.

She comes down to the pool with the girl limping behind her. "Sit down here," she says to the girl. "Here on this rock. This is a holy place." Then she squats down in the shallow water and washes the dirt from the girl's feet and legs. She pours water from the little blue pot, and in the dark they wash themselves.

Then they sit on the flat stones. Miriam hears the girl weeping, and for comfort's sake she holds her hands and tells her stories of the rooster and the fox, the leopard and the clever dog. She tells her stupid stories from the land of Egypt, until three women come and lead them to a fire, and give them wooden bowls of beet root and crushed artichoke. They have a separate encampment from their men. They sit with their faces uncovered, and sing songs of the one Christ, king of the house of David, born in Bethlehem to a poor woman.

Miriam and the girl sit quietly as the women talk. Laughing, they describe their men, crouched around the far end of the pool, not daring to look up. Mary of Magdala has been known to appear naked, clothed only in her red hair and a light which punishes men's eyes.

The woman are from Chorazin in Galilee, a town Miriam knows. But she says nothing. Instead she listens as they describe the food they laid out among the rocks that evening. On a stone table they laid out loaves of bread, and salted fish, and plates of beans and garlic, and even pieces of lamb roasted in honey and almonds, whatever they could afford and more. In the morning the food will be gone, they say, the dishes broken. They know it already, because this isn't the first time they've come. Not one has ever caught a glimpse of the mad woman, nor have they tried. Not one has ever ventured to the black mouth of the cave under its broken pediment. Stone images lie broken on the way.

Miriam and the girl sleep side by side among the rocks, wrapped in their shawls because the night is cold. They are wakened before dawn by biting gnats. They sit in the hollowed sand, rubbing their eyes, and the three women pass them to draw water at the pool's edge. As the sun rises the women squat in their wet shawls, praying for comfort. They catch the first light of the sun in a stream of water from a metal cup. They list their complaints, those of their children and friends. This is the reason they've come, this tiny ritual.

But Miriam and the girl climb to the south end of the valley to the cave. The rocks are tinged with pink. Some have been shaped and then later defaced by the blows of a hammer. There are toppled columns, a wide flight of steps. And then there's Mary of Magdala in a gray dress belted with hemp, sitting among the rocks. If she sees them, at first she gives no sign.

Even after all these years, Miriam finds herself muttering a charm against the wandering eye. But then she stops, awed by the look of this woman whom she hated once, a beggar on the roads, and yet so proud. She'd taken Jeshua away and many others just by a trick of her weakness, her face, her arms.

Miriam had thought to see her fierce and wild now, calling upon God. She's not prepared for the simple dress, the red hair tied back, streaked now with early gray. She's not ready for the calm face hardened by sorrow, from which all weakness and madness have disappeared.

She wants to be cruel, herself. But now she feels a softness, and before she can hesitate, she's climbed the steps and put her crippled hands around the shoulders of this woman who doesn't move, who isn't crying as she's crying, and yet who recognizes her suddenly. Then they're embracing and kissing each other, two women mourning the death of the thing they loved, though it's a long time ago now, six years.

Mary of Magdala brings them up a flight of steps in the middle of the tumbled rocks. She gives them bread and water in the shadow of a boulder away from the sun, which has turned hot now, though it's still early. They sit looking over the valley, over the pilgrims' tents. "They've come to see you," Miriam says, but Mary shakes her head.

"I've told my story many times."

They sit together at the top of the steps, which end under a heap of yellow stones. Now their first feelings are past and they are hesitant and embarrassed, Miriam thinks, both remembering past insults. The girl stands below them, and it's she who breaks the silence: "Why do you live here?"

Mary of Magdala says nothing, and the girl goes on. "Since my father's death and my brother's sickness, the house belongs to us. My sister and me. You would be welcome."

Miriam never imagined she thought of the house as hers. She goes on to describe Bethany—"There's a garden and some fields—no, of course. You've been there."

Mary of Magdala shakes her head. "I left of my own choice. I wasn't chased away."

She speaks with a soft awkwardness, because her first language is Greek. Listening to her, Miriam remembers an irritation six years old. She feels it suddenly, a pain under her heart. She says, "My son's death has made you what you are."

"I am nothing," the woman answers after a pause.

Which irritates Miriam still more—"People come all the way from Chorazin to wash in the water here. They bring you lamb cooked in onions for the sake of those lies. You and Bargiona."

Again the woman is silent. Miriam imagines she hasn't spoken for a long time. "Bargiona is a liar. That is true," she says, finally. "As for the meat, I leave it for the animals."

She forms silent words between her lips. And then—"You saw me the same morning."

"Hunh."

"Yes, but you knew. And I'm telling you. I thought he was the gardener."

On the first day of the week, after Jeshua died, Miriam went to Joseph's tomb in Aceldama where the dead are buried. She found Mary of Magdala lying on her back, dazed and sick from eating grass. She'd had a fit. There was blood on her lips.

Miriam feels a prickling on her hands. "You stupid girl, you never said a word to me. If you'd said something . . . " Miriam had led her to Joanna's house in the city, where they'd slept. In the evening Mary had gone to find Simon Bargiona and his brother, and started this nonsense.

"I'm telling you now," she says. "You never welcomed me into your house, though I was your daughter, your son's wife. You never gave me a kind word. Why should I have trusted you?"

She looks out over the dry valley and the pool. There's no madness in her eyes, which are gray, rimmed with a darker color. "It's a simple story. I saw two princes dressed as the centurions of Pilate's guard, standing beside the rock. When I climbed down, they were gone. The seal was turned aside. I stooped down to go in and heard his voice. When I turned back I saw him, though I didn't know him, for my eyes were closed. I asked him where he'd taken my husband's body, so I could tend to him as he deserved. And then he touched me and spoke to me."

It must have been the gardener after all, thinks Miriam. This is a woman who can't tell one man from another, she thinks, but doesn't say it. Instead—"Now Bargiona is drinking snake venom and healing the sick. My son appeared to twelve of them and fifty others, more each day, here and in Galilee. But you gave them the thought to do it. Bargiona's a rich man."

The woman shrugs as if to say, "But what I know, I know."

She's eaten nothing. Miriam has torn out chunks of the soft bread and shared it with the girl, who gives thanks to God. The water's in a clay pot with a broken rim.

Now the girl lifts up the pot and drinks. "You'd have your own place to sleep under the roof," she says. "Your own bed. For the rabbi's sake."

Mary of Magdala looks at her. "How is your brother, Lazarus? Whom the rabbi raised."

"She doesn't have another," Miriam says. She feels a rush of anger, partly because of this "rabbi" foolishness, partly because Lazarus is not well, never can be well. But the girl interrupts, smiling.

"He sits to eat."

She doesn't mention how he must be swaddled like a baby, how she washes out his linen four times every day. Miriam rubs her hands together. Her cheeks are full of bread, but she spits it out to talk—"You know what you know. This is what I know. Claudia Procula, the governor's wife, gave me a ring from her finger because she pitied me. I begged her on my knees. I sold the ring for thirty silver pieces and bought a place in Joseph's tomb in Aceldama, where I could lay out my son's body according to the law. We risked our lives to steal him from the tree, but when we saw you with the soldiers, I changed my mind. I thought you might reveal the place, so instead we brought him through Ge-hinnon in a wheelbarrow—his brothers, my cousin Salome, this girl, and me. It took us all night. Toward dawn we came to Bethany and laid him in Lazarus's place—the tomb at the bottom of the garden, where he still lies. We rubbed him with oil, and washed his wounds, and cried over him, and you weren't there. After one year we made the second burial and put his bones in the stone box. All spring and summer, every night I walk down there and light a lamp. My daughter has a house in Galilee, and I was with her for a little while, but I won't go again. I'll die with my son. Jeshua was my first-born, as you know."

While she talks, Miriam can see the men breaking up their tents in the bottom of the valley. There are four small donkeys, and a boy has taken them to drink by the pool. He's got a long stick, and he stands with the water around his legs. He's tied a ring of cloth around his head. Now he takes it off, soaks it in the water, puts it back.

Six more pilgrims climb down through the yellow rocks at the far side of the valley. A woman steps out from the shelter of a boulder beside the path, and embraces one of the newcomers. They know each other, Miriam thinks.

How hard it is to seize the truth, she thinks, to hold it in your hands. You can be angry for a moment, and then it drifts away. Or you're overtaken by other feelings, because she suddenly remembers how she felt about this young woman, how sometimes she longed to take her in her arms and shelter her against Jeshua, against the world. It is true that Jeshua abandoned her for months together, left her without money in the house of people who despised her. She has a beauty Miriam longs to touch, even still, with her aching hands. Her gray eyes, her fine nose, her white skin.

"He was my husband," murmurs the woman now, staring down from where she crouches on the topmost broken step. "I don't expect you to understand. Nothing I could ever do could please you.

"You turned him against me," she continues without bitterness, after a while.

But this is stupid, Miriam thinks. Jeshua never listened to what anyone said. If he'd followed her advice, he'd be alive.

"It was a long time ago," she says.

She reaches up to touch the woman's foot, because now she feels heavy with sadness and failure. The memory of that awful night is with her, how they carried the stiffening corpse. Her son had been a fine strong man, after his father. But that night she had cursed his weight. They'd had to drag him over the stones. When they brought him to the barrow and loaded him in, always a part of him, a leg or an outstretched arm, had spilled over the side. They never could find the balance, and when they left the road she'd had to walk in front through the ravine, clearing away branches and rocks.

She remembers the creak of the wooden axle. Often the barrow would tip over in the sand, and she would have to lift her son up by his naked leg and fling him in. His arm had stiffened from his body with the shape of the cross. His fingers poked out through the ripped shroud. Or when she took hold of the barrow's rim, there was his shoulder, pale and greasy in the moonlight.

They'd hid in the bushes and among the dry thistles. The wheel creaked and creaked. When they got inside the gate at Bethany there was something else, some other terrible thing, Simon the leper's body, smooth without a mark, lying in the store room. What crushing spirit had Jeshua sent out of the land of death?

Miriam doesn't turn her head to look, but she wonders if the girl below her on the stairs is thinking of that night. If so, what does she see? Does she see her father laid out on his back, his face quiet as if asleep? Or is it Jeshua she sees, always Jeshua, as they carried him through the garden and turned back the seal from Lazarus's tomb?

"It's a long time ago," Miriam says again. But it's not long. Six years is like six days. That night is in her bones. She lives with it as they all do. If Jeshua's ghost visited Mary of Magdala as she lay in the wrong tomb, was that so strange? If he told her not to look for him in that place?

When Miriam stole the corpse down from the tree, when she gave her money to Joseph of Arimathea, when she dragged her son to Bethany in the cold night, it was to close the gate of Sheol over his head. But now he knocked on all their doors. If she'd let the soldiers drag him out into the rocks and leave him for the pigs and the wild dogs, his spirit might have rested quieter.

"Once I saw him, too," Miriam says. Why has she come here? Why is she sitting on these steps among the rocks as the sun climbs the sky? The shade is almost gone.

She'd thought she might tell the woman, "Stop your lies." Ask her to take the story back, once she knew the truth. Harm had been done in Jeshua's name. Maybe she might have told her about Sapphira and her murdered husband. But now Miriam finds herself describing a dream, how she woke in the night to find Jeshua beside her. He knelt down to grasp her hands, but when she asked him a question, he was gone.

She'd never told anyone about this, because she was afraid she might cry. Besides, it's a small thing, compared to the lies she's heard. But now she does cry as she remembers her son's face, how the light had shone on his wounded head. What light? There was no lamp, no window.

There's nothing to tell, yet the tears are on her face. As always, weakness makes her cruel. "You stupid whore," she says to Mary of Magdala on the steps. "Why couldn't you leave my son in peace? You," she continues, speaking now to the girl, Mary of Bethany, who stands below her in the open sun. "You're just the same. How could you let him touch you?" she says, meaning Thaddeus the Galilean. "His father was a shoemaker."

The girl turns her face away, red as if Miriam had slapped her. "She was grunting like a pig over those bags of grain," Miriam says, though it's a lie. "Sapphira they had to beat to get her legs apart." She blows her nose between her forefinger and thumb. Nothing but tears and greasy dust, which she wipes on her dress.

"You left me alone," says the girl.

But Miriam can't bear to hear her say it. "Stupid whore," she mutters, though she is sure Thaddeus did not harm her. He would not have had the courage, she tells herself. The stones burn in the sun. She clambers to her feet. But Mary of Magdala has grabbed hold of her sleeve. She tries to pull away, but loses her balance and falls down. Who is this woman? she thinks, panicked suddenly. These years in the desert have made her strong. When Jeshua was alive she used to follow after him, prone to fits and weak hysteria. Now women come from Chorazin to see her. Miriam is the weak one now, an old woman full of tears and shame. What help, what protection can she give?

The sun burns above the pinnacles of rock. Below her, women carry goat skins of water from the pool. "When we were in Ge-hinnon, he fell out," she says. "We had to load him into the barrow like a sack of onions. All the way we'd smelled the smoke, but when we came around the corner into Kidron, the city was on fire. It was burning behind the valley wall. And his white hand came out, the fingers splayed apart.

Then I laid him in the tomb, and that pig Simon, too, below him in the alcove. After a year I put his bones in the stone box."

Now the girl, Simon's second daughter, has turned back and is staring up at her. And Mary of Magdala has her by the sleeve. "Come with me," she says.

The calmness is gone out of her face, and Miriam is grateful. She can't stop talking. "I gave thirty drachmae to my cousin Joseph, but he wanted more. He came to Golgotha later that night, but my sons beat him, chased him away. We had nothing more to give."

And it was Joseph, she was now convinced, who had betrayed them, so that the Romans sent their soldiers to the empty tomb. "That night there was God's curse on the whole world for my son's sake. Simon the leper was struck down."

Four crows sit below her on the rocks. They're picking at the crumbs of bread. Mary of Magdala isn't listening. Instead she pulls her by the sleeve. "Come with me out of the sun," she says, and now Miriam can see the entrance to the cave set into the red wall of the cliff. It stands in plain sight among the broken piles of masonry, but she hasn't noticed it until this moment. The steps lead up to it, though they are covered in places by the sliding stones.

There's nothing wrong with her knees, and she gets up. She allows Mary of Magdala to lead her like a donkey. And it's true she feels better when she's out of the light, inside the sudden coolness of the cave's mouth. There is the smell of bats. There is the high ceiling cleft in the red rock, the polished corner where Mary lives. There is her mat, her broom, her dish, her water pot, her books, lit from the side through a square window high above. There is where she sleeps, a bed of rushes on the cold red stone. Scratched with a sharp rock beside it, a row of letters which Miriam can't read.

Later she'll tell herself she was mistaken and she couldn't have seen, deeper in a recess of the cave, the stone statue of the bull, head split apart, horns broken short. She couldn't have seen the procession of bulls and dancers cut into the wall. Now she doesn't care, as Jeshua's widow makes her sit on the straw bed, fusses over her, washes her face. She imagines she might lie down forever in the cool bat smell. But Mary of Magdala is bending over her holding a cup of water. "The sun is very strong," she says. "Now tell me. It wasn't just to call us whores that you came all this way."

* * *

But it was just for that, as it turned out.

For six years Miriam has cursed Jeshua's widow for a liar—cursed her not to others, but to herself. But if the woman did see what she claims, what then?

Coming from Bethany, Miriam thought that she could shame Jeshua's widow for the girl's sake. She hoped Mary of Magdala would come down from her cave and tell the truth. Surely men would listen and the truth would sap the strength of Simon Bargiona and Thaddeus the zealot. Instead it would give strength to Thomas Didymus, and Judas Sicarius, and Jacob, her son.

But as she lies on Mary's bed, she feels the moment pass. It was Bargiona who bowed down to her, called her the mother of the risen Christ. Though she is angry about Sapphira, and the girl, and the money Bargiona stole, is she prepared to give that up? Now she feels her anger cool, and she imagines that her only power is in the lie. If she takes Stephen of Antioch and others to the tomb at the bottom of the garden, and shows them Jeshua's bones, and tells them the story of his death, would they believe her?

No, the lie has too much strength, she tells herself, and any strength she has depends on it. Besides, it had done good as well as harm. Without the lie, she tells herself, Simon the leper's cousins will take back the house in Bethany.

So in the afternoon they return home, she and the girl. The sun is hot, and they are thirsty the whole way. Once Miriam climbs to a cleft above the road, and they crouch between the boulders to watch men on horseback ride from Jericho, a hundred at least. They don't stop or turn, but continue toward the city in a cloud of red dust. They are carrying the flag of the tenth legion, the wild pig.

"You be quiet. Now come on," Miriam says

But houses have been burned in Bethany, broken apart, the beams still smoking. There are broken pots. The street's deserted, though it's early evening, past the heat of the day. In the doorways, no lights shine. Sometimes a curtain stirs, but no one calls to them. Miriam knows no one in the town. The women won't speak to her. Their husbands have forbidden it.

Miriam turns the corner of the street and the girl follows her. When she sees them Martha comes out through the gate. She takes her sister by her hands and kisses them. "Oh," she says, "Sapphira is dead during the night."

Then they cross into the safety of the yard. "What's this?" asks Miriam, pointing to a broken bed outside the gate.

"Hush. It's about Caesar's statue. Rachel's house caught fire."

The emperor Caligula has commanded his statue to be raised in Herod's temple and the priests to offer sacrifices. That year there has been fighting in Jerusalem. Martha says, "Jews were beaten and the soldiers were attacked. Oh, I'm glad to see you. Sapphira bled during the night and then she died."

"Were there soldiers here?" asks the girl.

Martha shakes her head. She has her by the hands, and she's pulling them into the house. "Come talk to me. Come into the house. Where have you been? I was so worried when you didn't come."

Later Miriam walks around the side of the barn to the store room where the dead woman is laid out on a low table among the bags of grain. She can't bring herself to ask whether Sapphira talked about her money at the end when she was dying. So now Miriam goes to look although there's nothing to see. Lamps burn at the woman's head and feet in the dark room. A message has gone out to her father. Sapphira was a childless widow. She asked for no one, Martha says, even as death came for her.

Miriam sits down beside the table on a wicker box. She's tired and her hands ache. There's a small ache in her tooth and her tongue finds it. The women have gone into the house and left her. Sarah the Egyptian is somewhere near. Miriam imagines she can hear her moving outside the door.

The Egyptian has bound up the corpse with linen strips. There's a cloth over the face, but the hands and feet are bare. Miriam sits humming to herself, moving her fingers in her lap. Now she's ashamed, and she can't bring herself to search the corpse. It makes her angry, but the money is gone. Soon the body must be taken up, taken away. She has nothing to say over this woman, murdered by her son's friends. Nor does she want this woman in the tomb at the bottom of the garden. That is her son's place.

But there's a common grave below the hill of Olives. Surely it's not too much to hope that someone will take this corpse away before the sun goes down. In the quiet store room she imagines that the street in Bethany is also quiet, that the soldiers of the tenth legion have brought a calmness to Jerusalem. What difference can it make if Gaius Caligula's statue stands in Nicanor's gate? The whole temple is a piss-pot of idol-worship, as her son once said.

These are her thoughts, and after an hour they subdue her, so she falls asleep. When she wakes, the darkness seems to have come closer, have settled in around her. And there's a noise in the room with her, a scurrying and scuffling. Rats among the bags, she thinks. She has slumped back against the wall, and for a while she sits without moving, confused, stiff, sore. Then she sees Lazarus has come.

He must have walked across the courtyard from the house. Now he steps out from the shadows, naked. He was a big man once. Now he's diminished, white, a ghost of himself. His back is bent, his head too heavy for his shoulders. His penis is shriveled up.

She sits without moving, watching him drag himself forward. He holds onto the lip of a wine jar, one of a line along the wall. He passes himself from rim to rim, steadying himself with his right hand until he comes into the open space at the back of the room. The corpse is set upon a wooden plank, held off the dirt by wooden stools.

Clay lamps burn at both ends of the plank, but they have dwindled down. There is no light from the doorway, no current of air. Miriam imagines the wooden door has been sealed shut. She's too old to be afraid, and so she sits motionless and watches Lazarus stagger on until he stands with both hands on the rim of the last jar. Then he sinks down to his hands and knees, crawls forward over the packed earth.

Now she hears he's saying something, crooning something to himself. But she can't make it out. And maybe it's just the rhythm of his breathing as he drags himself toward the corpse. He's so close below her, his knee brushes her skirt. If she stretched out her foot, she could push him over, make him fall.

At the edge of the plank he reaches up to touch the woman's shroud. He starts to pull himself up by the edge of the plank. Miriam can't look at him. Instead she stares at the dead woman, and for the first time she sees something. The woman's hands are crossed over her breast, and Miriam can see there's something in her left hand, a talisman, a piece of baked clay. She's made up her mind to get up from her seat, and she's thinking of the words to make Lazarus go, make him stop fumbling for the death her son denied him. But then she feels the air from the open door, and Martha and the girl are there, though she hasn't heard them coming. Martha has a stick. She brings it up above her head.

"Stop," Miriam says. "Don't touch him. This is his house."

She gets to her feet. It makes her angry to imagine how they think she needs protecting, an old woman who has fallen asleep, and Lazarus has come upon her in the dark. "This is his house, not yours." It makes her angry to see the woman raise her stick against her brother. As long as he's alive, they can pay his workers, eat his food, sleep in his beds.

Some men have come, too. They stand at the mouth of the store room, hesitating to come in. They have come to fetch the body. How can Martha be so stupid, to let them see her with the stick? Miriam falls to her knees. She puts her crippled hands on Lazarus's shoulders, and the girl, Mary, is there too. Weeping, she raises him up, leaving Miriam to stare at the dead woman's hand, at the clay talisman clutched in the dead fingers. No one is watching. She plucks it out, hides it in her belt.

Why? She imagines it might be a clue, a message about the seven hundred drachmae that Sapphira promised them. Later on her bed, she lights a candle to look at it: the clay figure of a woman, her body pierced with nails. Nails pierce the woman's mouth and breasts and belly. The clay is soft, unfired, and it breaks apart under Miriam's clumsy hands, showing the lead tablet it contains inside its body. She unfolds it into four leaves, and gazes at the rows of letters in the Greek alphabet, unknown to her, although she recognizes some of the shapes.

She has heard of such things. In the land of Egypt, people give messages to the care of murdered corpses, who are their couriers to the lord of the dead.

That night she sits on her bed of rushes in her small, windowless room. She can't sleep. The girl Mary lies in another corner on her blanket, and as always she sleeps deeply, stretched out motionless on her back.

In the morning someone comes. Miriam is sitting at the bottom of the garden. There's a block of stone Martha had cut for her. Three men dragged it down so she could sit like this beside her son's tomb, where it rises out of the earth. Now as always in the morning she sits watching the sky turn pink, the chalk-like stones turn pink. When she sees a man in the bean field, she hopes it's the boy, Stephen of Antioch. Maybe he'll forgive an old woman for being so rude. She would be happy to see his face. "I came to see if you were safe," he says.

But it's not he. It's another man who comes to see her sometimes, an ugly man, a cripple. At first she can't remember his name. He's dressed in the Greek fashion, and she looks at his strong legs, his linen cloak trimmed with a purple stripe. He stands above her. Most of her visitors would squat or sit before her in the dust, but he won't. He's the kind of man Jeshua hated, the son of a rich citizen of Rome, a Jew who made his money selling tents to the twelfth legion. Now she remembers. His name is Saul, though lately he has taken a Roman name. He's from Tarsus. He's left his servants at the gate, she's sure.

She shakes her head. "My fingers give me pain, especially in the morning. There's a prickling in the joints, and then I can't feel anything . . . "—she would have gone on, except she sees him frown and glance over his shoulder. He has the whitest, smoothest, palest skin she's ever seen. His lips are pale, his eyes rimmed with red. He has no beard. The hair on his head is almost white, though he's not old.

"There was fighting here," he says. "I was afraid for you."

But she thinks, who would bother an old woman? She asks about the city. "Is there a fire? I saw the soldiers pass."

Then, "Is someone dead?" she asks. "I heard some of the Romans have taken our side."

This is what she's heard: Gaius Caesar, whom the soldiers call Caligula, has made a golden statue of himself. He's sent it to Israel with orders to have it placed inside the temple. Petronius, the Roman governor, has refused, because he fears the anger of the Jews. The statue stands at the dock in Caesarea, still crated up. "They must be afraid of us," she mumbles, "to disobey their king."

But he won't say anything about that. "There is someone dead," he says. "You're right."

So that's it. He has something to tell her. She waits for it. She's sitting next to her son's tomb, which is faced in blocks of stone. The sun has come up over the wall, which pleases her because her feet are cold. She's watching Saul of Tarsus's beardless face, his bloodless lips.

He stands in front of her and she looks at his strong knees. "Let me explain," he says. "I have no patience with these fools. Nazorites, zealots—I hate them. These riots and disturbances against our laws. When Tiberius Caesar was alive, then we had peace," he says, then pauses again.

When she looks up, his eyes are liquid, bright. "But I tell you, I had a dream. I saw Jeshua of Nazareth in his own flesh. I asked his name." And then he goes on to repeat what he's already told her more than once, how Jeshua called him on the Damascus road.

It angers Miriam that men who never knew her son can recognize his voice, his ghost. As if he haunted all the roads, when before God she knows he's lying in the tomb not ten steps from where she sits. She interrupts—"Who's been killed? Is it Thomas Didymus?"

He frowns, but can't be stopped. "When I was in Damascus, I thought, 'I will go search out his family and the students who were with him. I will search out Simon Peter bar Jonah and the sons of Zebedee.' Now I've tried to close my eyes, but they are evil men, as you know."

"Some of them," Miriam says.

"Your son was a prince of the house of David through his father, Joseph the carpenter. But they are peasants and illiterates. Two nights ago and last night there were riots in the town because of Caesar's statue. Simon Peter bar Jonah was their leader, and Thaddeus the zealot—they attacked the soldiers on the archway, as they did the week your son was crucified. They indulge their love of fighting, and all Jews suffer. Now more than ever, when our governor has risked his life, we should stand with him. This Roman is not like Pontius Pilate.

He is a brave man, and God has chosen him to protect Israel. You were there in the afternoon in Bar Jonah's house. You saw the preparations for the fight."

She shrugs, embarrassed because she saw nothing, understood nothing. Why is Saul of Tarsus telling her these things?

"I wasn't there," he says. "If I'd known, I would have warned the captain of the guard. Now more than ever, we must be calm."

Miriam has been looking for his infirmity, which he seldom shows. But now he's gesturing with his right hand, and for a moment she sees his left hand too. It comes out of his wide sleeve, thin and white, with two fingers and no thumb. "You have influence with them," he says. "You and the other one whom they call Cleopas's wife. Last night that man Thaddeus was boasting about her, and Thomas Didymus was angry. He beat him with his fists. He said he'd come to find you, because he remembers you from the old days and the other Mary too. Now, what I want to know is, has he come here? Did he give something to you?"

"Tell me who was killed."

The man doesn't look at her. "For your son's sake, I'll tell. Thomas Didymus struck Thaddeus the zealot on the cheeks and cursed him. Then he walked out and some went with him. So Bar Jonah went before the crowd and told them a new story, how your son appeared to them after his death and only Didymus denied him. In the evening they knocked him down outside the house, beat him with sticks, chased him away. Then they went out with torches to set fires and throw stones at the soldiers in the Xystus."

As he speaks, she finds she has taken from her belt the lead tablet from Sapphira's hand. She has unfolded the heavy leaves. And she's bending them around her fingers, wrapping her old hands with it. Why? She can't say. But she thinks maybe the lead has a healing nature—she's heard something of the kind. Surely it's a strange metal, the way it takes a shape, then keeps it. Saul is looking at her now as if he wants something. He says, "Thomas Didymus was going to challenge Peter bar Jonah for the leadership of the synagogue. He had spoken to me, and your son Jacob was with him. He had a sign he was giving to his followers. But when he heard about Thaddeus and the woman, he forgot himself. He moved too soon."

She says nothing, and he continues: "Did he talk to you? Did he give you some sort of token? You have strength over these men for your son's sake. If he is in danger now, then you can help him."

She's thinking about Thomas Didymus, who loved her son. It's scarcely a day since she saw him in Jerusalem and on the road. The boy gave her a blue pot. But now for some reason she can't bring their faces to mind. She sits crumpling the lead paper and then smoothing it out, hoping it will ease the stiffness in her joints.

Saul of Tarsus says, "Now I wanted to tell you that I heard Bar Jonah talking to the crowd about Judas ish Keriot, whom you've mentioned. Bar Jonah says he was the one who sold your son to Pontius Pilate for thirty drachmae and used it to buy a piece of land in Aceldama—you know because if one was a traitor, then the rest must have been faithful. All they talk about is which of them your son loved best."

"Sicarius," Miriam says. "Ish Keriot was someone else."

She thinks how hard the stone is under her old backside. How she wishes the man would go. She feels sick to her stomach and her bladder is full. She says: "Sicarius spent more than thirty drachmae on the land, and then there was the house too. And the orchard. Have you seen the place? He wasn't like the rest of them—he got the money from his father."

Then in a moment she continues. "Ish Keriot was someone else. He was Pilate's spy, and he was with the Romans when they took my son. These people know the difference."

"You ask if you can do something for me," she says a moment later. "There is one thing. I can't read the letters on this piece of paper. Can you read them for me?"

She unwraps the lead paper from her wrist. She holds it out to him and he squats down to take it. Doubtless he thinks it is the message from Thomas Didymus. Now she can see his left hand clearly as he uses it to smooth out the words. She watches his lips move, and then he says, "Where did you get this?"

"I took it from Sapphira of Jericho's dead hand. You know she was robbed and beaten, and her husband too."

She feels an anger in herself, a rage about to burst. She imagines putting her hand on his smooth high pale forehead. In her mind she pushes him over into the dust. The dust stains his white cloak with the purple trim.

He's angry too, she notices. His small, plucked eyebrows have come together over his nose. He's mumbling to himself, making the sign of the evil eye. He drops the tablet as if the metal cut his fingers. Then he snatches it up, crumples it into a ball as he rises to his feet. He throws it to a corner of the yard—"What are you doing here?" he says when he can speak. "What are you doing here? Mother, this is not the place for you. Come with me now, and I will take you to your family's house in Sepphoris."

After he's gone, she sits for a while in the sun. She leans her back against the mud wall, and maybe she falls asleep. Is it a dream now that the girl, her namesake, comes to her? She comes to lead her inside out of the hot sun. She stands in front of her. And Miriam says, "Go fetch that piece of metal paper and read me the words. How long has that black girl lived here? I mean Sarah, who's your sister's slave." And Mary goes into the corner and comes back with the crumpled leaves. She sits down on the bench to push them flat. With many frowns and bad starts, she begins to read. It's the Egyptian herself who has been teaching her.

"'Darkness,'" she says, "'three-headed dog, and you the traveler, Sapphira, Helen's daughter, now in the house of Anubis and the kings of earth, on your knees give them my message. You spirit driver with your stinging whip, inflame the heart, the liver of Martha, whom Leah bore, now, quickly, quickly. Drag her by her hair, her inward tongue until she no longer stays apart from me. Make her a slave to me for the entire time of my life, filled with love, speaking all the things of her heart. Inflame her with love for Sarah Sarapias, daughter of Isara. By her liver, her belly, her inward lips, drag her to the bath house at Bethany, and you, become a bath-woman. Burn her with love for Sarapias, Isara's daughter, and burn her body day and night until she goes under like a slave, giving herself and all she has, because this is the will of Jehovah, the great God. I ask you by the secret symbols to drag Martha, Leah's daughter, into the bath house at Bethany. And you, become the servant of the bath, and join us together there. The bed of Persephone delights you, who knows the secret symbols Enor thenor Abrasax peuchre Phre Arsenophre abari mamarembo iao iaboth—honey-finder, honey gatherer, honey-giver, burn and scourge her till she comes into the bath house to find relief, and cools her body in the water.'"

* * *

Except where she stutters, or puzzles over the sound, Mary's voice is slow and flat as if she read a list of numbers or receipts. She's not troubled by the meaning of the words. Or else she doesn't understand them. Later, lying on her bed in the hot afternoon, Miriam questions her own memory. Perhaps a spirit came when she was asleep and whispered in her ear. Where's the lead tablet now? Where has it gone?

As often happens she has woken with an image of Jeshua in her mind. There he is, talking with his hand raised. Or he is just looking at her. As always in her mind, asleep or awake, she's pushing him away, turning stubbornly to other thoughts because what's the profit there? Each glimpse of him is like a wound. Now she's woken on her own bed in her airless, windowless hole, and she stares tenaciously at the beams and plaited wicker a few feet above her head. She doesn't remember coming in or lying down. But she finds herself listening to the creaks of the house, the insects in the walls, searching for the sound of the Egyptian in the small rooms. She listens for the noise of a curtain drawn back or high-arched footsteps on the dirt floor. And at the same time she's thinking about Judas Sicarius the pot maker, her son's friend.

Or she's thinking about everything that Saul of Tarsus told her. The fate of women is to be ignorant, she thinks. Now there are riots in the city and a fight over the statue: whether to resist the Roman governor or support him. The members of Jeshua's synagogue have taken sides against each other: Simon Bargiona and Thaddeus and the zealots on one side, Thomas Didymus and her son Jacob on the other.

But what about Judas Sicarius? How does he fit in? He had some money from his father and he bought a house outside the village of Aceldama, north of the city on the Joppa road. He chose the place because of where it was, a sabbath-day's walk from the city of the dead where Joseph of Arimathea had his tomb. He used to go often to the place, because he thought Jeshua was raised there out of Sheol. Miriam had not told him the truth. There was a brightness in his eyes when he talked about her son.

What harm does it do, if he is mistaken? she'd thought. Judas lived in Aceldama with his wife and two young sons. He no longer spoke of war, of killing soldiers. But he made pots with a blue glaze and sold them from his shop. Nor did he speak much to the others after Jeshua's death.

Why do they hate him? she wonders now. Maybe because of his blue eyes and red hair. Because he left them to make a life of his own. Or for the money his father gave him. He wasn't like them, fishermen and beggars. He could read and write. His father worked his own land near Bethsaida.

Miriam lies on her back in the stifling half-light, listening for the sound of the Egyptian's step. But she's thinking about Sicarius. After she came back from her daughter's husband's house in Sepphoris, in Galilee, Judas Sicarius would visit her. Always he'd bring money or small gifts, a piece of dyed cloth, a pot, a lamb sausage. They'd sit talking about this and that. Now he has the dropsy and can't walk—why do they hate him? Why do they call him by the name of Pilate's spy? John of Zebedee knows the difference. He stabbed that old man, Judas ish Keriot in the dark, killed him, cut off his ear. Maybe he doesn't like to remember.

She listens for a noise in the house, anything, a rat crossing the floor. But she hears nothing. Then suddenly she's afraid of the silence and she starts up. Maybe now, she thinks, now at this moment they are at the bath house where Martha goes to wash herself after her flow of blood. Or maybe now they're in the shed close by at the back of the house, where there's water in the big pot.

She can't stand up because she'll hit her head. Instead she goes down on her knees beside the pallet of rushes and she reaches under the linen cloth. She thrusts her hand into the straw and pulls out her small bag of coins which she has hidden there. As she does every morning when she wakes, every night when she lies down, she empties the bag into the dirt to count her money. Even in the darkness she can do it.

She knows the shape of each coin. Often she lingers over this work, because though her hands are clumsy, she enjoys the feel of the money, the thin copper pieces, the heavy silver drachmae. But now she counts them hurriedly, afraid that the Egyptian has robbed her while she slept—no, no. Everything's there.

Relieved, she sits down on the floor, then leans her back against the pallet. A small light comes from the chinks in the stone wall. She sprawls back on her elbows. Someone has loosened the front of her shirt, and the cloth falls away. Dressing and undressing before light, after dark, she never sees herself, and now she looks down without recognition at her own body, her bony chest, her flat and sunken breasts. Her skin is gray and loose, and now she touches herself with her clumsy fingertips, running them along the grooves between her ribs.

The image of her son comes to her. There is laughter on his big lips, and she turns away. What day is it? Is it the week of the atonement now? No, no, she must be dreaming. How could she be so stupid? The spring has come, and soon it will be passover time. But once when she was just a girl, she saw the ceremony of the two goats on the day of the atonement. The first was taken to the altar to be killed, and the other was pulled through the streets by a red rope while people cursed it and spat at it and threw stones, and loaded it with sins, and drove it out into the dry hills. When she was young, she'd cried and could not be consoled. Now she has no tears. "You sons of whores," she mutters as she pushes her purse of coins down into the inside pocket of her dress. She reaches again into the straw, and pulls out the blue pot with the heavy glaze, which Judas Sicarius's servant gave her on the road. This must be the sign that Saul of Tarsus mentioned. Then she crawls out on her hands and knees past the palm mat where the girl sleeps, onto the tiled floor beside the washing shed, and she can stand upright.

Now her ears are unsealed, and she can hear the noises of the house. She hears Lazarus coughing on his bed. She hears the thump of the grinding stone. The girl is kneeling under the low roof that extends on wooden posts from the house into the kitchen yard. Standing inside the wash room door, watching her work, Miriam remembers the feel of the pitted stone, the pain in her back—it's been years now since she was strong enough. When she was at the stone, it was always with a head as empty as a sheep's, but this girl is singing. The sound of her singing has led Miriam from inside the house. She stands beside the post of the wash room door, tying the strings of her shirt, retying her rope belt. She thrusts the blue pot into her breast, where she can feel the bulge of it. All the time she's listening to the small song, and watching the girl on her knees under the low, thatched roof. She lifts the stone and pulls it back, and sets it into the trough, and pushes it down away from her over the grains of wheat. Her hands, her face, her neck are white from the dust, sticking to her sweat. She has tied her long hair back, but a strand of it escapes over her cheek.

Miriam listens to the song, a small, light-hearted, wordless thing. The girl's eyes are large and dark against the white dust on her face, and the lines of her brows come together. Is she thinking about the words of the lead tablet? Or about Thaddeus the zealot who attacked her in the dark, while Miriam did nothing?

Now the song stops. The girl pauses in her work, and she's looking at the doorway. So Miriam steps out of it and stands in the open air. "Where's the black Egyptian?" she says, but the girl doesn't answer. She's smaller than her sister Martha, without Martha's big shoulders, strong breasts and thighs. She was already a woman—twelve years old—when Jeshua died. But always she seems a child to Miriam, because of her slimness and because she has no man. A child who won't grow up—Miriam's daughter is not much older and she has children of her own.

"I'm going to Aceldama," she says. Then, "Where's your sister?" but she doesn't want to know. She turns away before the girl can speak, murmuring a curse on this house of childless women, and she thinks to herself as she walks through the gate that she won't come again. She'll take her money and follow Saul of Tarsus up to Galilee, and she'll live there with her daughter's husband or her son Simon. She can be there in three days. Not that they'd be glad to have her, and she'll have to work there, she knows, and she won't be able to sit all morning under the sycamore tree, or sleep in the afternoon like a doddering old slave who has outlived her usefulness.

What has happened to Thomas Didymus? And Judas Sicarius is in danger—she is sure of it. She has a long way to go, to Aceldama north of the city. And so she hurries down the street past the burned house. Men are picking through the rubble. They turn and stare as she goes by with her face uncovered, her shawl flapping. There are soldiers at the well, and she makes the sign of the evil eye, muttering to herself and thinking if she ever once crossed the threshold of her son's house in Galilee, she'd never leave. There'd be no place for her to go. Nor would there be any meat for her, or wine, or white bread, or honey cakes. Her sons are poor men with children to feed. Mary and Martha have been kind to her.

She crosses over the shoulder of the hill of Olives, then goes into the valley under the walls of Jerusalem. There's water in the stream bed now, the Kidron river. When she reaches it, she turns north and follows the road past Herod's wall.

Judas Sicarius once brought her a silver denarius. She still has it in her bag, one of nine. One morning he'd walked from Aceldama with his new wife—she had a broken tooth filed smooth. She'd smiled much and said nothing. He'd asked Miriam to come live with him in Aceldama, where she could be close to Jeshua's tomb. He'd asked her to go with him that same afternoon, and when she shook her head, he seemed doubtful, hurt. "Because I know my son's not there," she'd said, which was the truth. He'd nodded, had looked up with trembling lips. He thought she was talking about something else, telling him her son had risen from the dead. At that moment he loved her. So how could she have told him the rest, about that night on Golgotha? And how could she have gone with him with that lie between them, even though she liked him, his freckled face, his sharp blue eyes.

When she buried her son in Bethany, the others asked her if she meant to tell his students where he lay. "If they were here, they'd know," she'd said. She'd made them swear they'd say nothing, because she was afraid of the Romans and their spies. Later, every time she thought to tell the truth to men like Thomas Didymus, or Judas Sicarius, or the sons of Zebedee, she'd thought—I can't. Or just a little longer. It's only because of this lie that they are talking to me, they are listening. Jeshua rose out of the tomb at Aceldama, and he's my son. Without that, I have nothing.

"I've broken with Bargiona," Judas had said. Among her son's students, one or two had taken Jeshua's death to mark the end of all that secrecy and fighting, the beginning of new lives. Even then, years ago, he'd told her how Bargiona had put out a rumor that he'd bought his land with Roman money. "He said I took thirty silver pieces from Asterius Agrippa to betray him and the sons of thunder. It was the money Judas ish Keriot was to have been paid."

Again, how could she tell him the truth? That she and Joanna had spoken to a servant of the temple, asking to trade Bargiona for her son's life. She'd known where he was hiding. But the Romans never made such bargains and besides, she was a woman. But maybe someone had stolen what she knew, taken it without paying. She'd heard Bargiona had escaped from the city with his life and nothing else, the same day her son was crucified. The soldiers had been close behind him. Four men had died. That day and every day, she would have done anything to save her son.

So she could only nod her head when Sicarius asked her, "Can you speak to him? The money was my father's. And the thirty silver pieces were what you paid for a place in Joseph of Arimathea's tomb."

Frightened and angry, she had shaken her head. "Claudia Procula gave me a ring from her finger. Pilate's wife gave me her ring because she pitied me, for the sake of her own stillborn child." This was something she had said so much that it was like the truth. "I sold it for thirty drachmae," she said. Even now, that sounds like the truth, and it's hard for her to remember how Joanna's husband—Herod's steward—had paid her the money with a puzzled frown. He'd paid the coins out one by one into her cupped hands, and never spoken to her again. She'd not asked him, but she hoped the money was his charity, because he was a rich man. But maybe it had come through Asterius Agrippa and Pilate's men—payment for Bargiona's life, though he had escaped. Thirty drachmae—she was happy to have spent them.

"I'll speak to Bargiona," she'd said to Judas Sicarius, but she had not.

Now the sun is low over the western hills. Out of breath, she pauses by a broken wall. She has passed men on the road, but no one has spoken to her. Now there are three boys who come sliding down the hill with sticks in their hands. In spite of everything the Romans do, there are still robbers in these dry hills north of the city. She feels the weight of her purse next to her skin. These boys are an evil, weak-boned, bandy-legged, ragged lot, sons of Samaritan whores she thinks, and they bow their heads and put out their right hands like beggars. She won't give them a single copper piece, she decides. Never in her life has she given money to a beggar.

So she marches past them and they follow her, sticks in their hands. Besides, she thinks, I can't show them my purse. She's frightened, because she's heard stories of women attacked in these places—who has not? And even though she's an old woman in a stained and mended dress, she imagines they might punish her just for the fun of it, knock her down onto the rocks, rip her clothes. So she turns back toward the largest boy, an underfed, bow-legged brute maybe twelve years old, and she grabs him by the ear. "I have nothing," she whispers, her teeth clenched. "Nothing at all."

When they have run away, she sits down on a stone beside the path. There was a house here once. Some big stones remain, part of an old wall. She sits catching her breath, and after a moment she begins to cry, a hoarse, dry, useless noise.

But it's a good life, she thinks, inside the wall at Bethany, where those women bring her food every afternoon, even the black woman whom she hates. They listen to her for her own sake, because of the life she gave them there, secure from men, with money of their own. Simon the leper's cousins would have taken everything.

Then for no reason she remembers the feast of the atonement when she was young, and she saw the goat led out to die with the red cloth around its horns. The men threw rocks, stabbed it with their sticks—what is this itching, this prickling in her hands, this pain in her shoulders? After a few minutes her breath comes easier, and she gets up.

The sun is setting as she comes to Aceldama. Here too the street is empty, and she imagines the people cowering in their dark rooms because of the fighting in the city. But there are no soldiers here, and only one shop is wrecked. The pots are broken on the ground. Only one house is burnt, a small house north of the town where Judas Sicarius lived with his family among the olive trees.

The sun is a red coin on the horizon as she limps into the yard. The smell of the fire sickens her, the sweet smell. Tables and stools have been dragged out and smashed. The roof is broken in. One wall is clean, and black words have been written on it, words which she can't read. The letters are as long as her arm, scratched with a charred stick on the red clay.

There's an olive tree behind the house. Its trunk is burned, its branches broken, and many of the leaves have been stripped away. Judas Sicarius hangs from a rope in the top branches. She goes and stands beneath him, watching his naked body turn, though there's no wind. In the past years he was sick with dropsy, and his legs are bloated, swollen, white. Flies crawl on them.

Sometimes he'd come to Bethany with his two brown-haired boys.

Because she feels the weight of it, she takes out her bag of coins and lays it among the roots of the tree, thirty drachmae and more. Then she turns to look over the broken wall, to peer inside the house but there is nothing. She finds the handle of an iron pot. It's sticking up out of the cinders.

Soon it will be dark. She finds a broken box and puts it against the tree trunk. She kicks it and then clambers onto it, the piece of metal in her hand, and she's climbing up into the tree when the men come. The branches are within reach. A child could climb this tree, but she's not strong enough. Her fingers are cold and shaking now. She warms them in her armpits, standing on the box and singing to herself. The corpse turns above her, the bloated, mottled flesh, and for comfort's sake she's singing to herself in her low voice, part of the prayers for the dead which are a woman's duty. She warms her fingers in her armpits, standing on the box and singing, muttering to herself until she hears the voices of the men, and she is quiet. Maybe they won't see her. She grips the iron handle in her fist.

The men have brought torches. She pushes her back against the tree trunk, watching the yellow light, whispering to herself. Then she feels a terrible relief when she recognizes her son Jacob among the men. Her second son. She hears his voice. They've come from among the olive trees, and now they're standing below her, and Jacob is looking up at her. Then he's reaching out his hand and saying, "Come down, woman. You are safe."

And in a little while, "Come down now."

And in a little while more, "Don't play the fool. Take my hand. Get down from there and let us take him down. Let these men do their work."

But she's afraid of him. He shakes his head. "Sicarius's wife is safe. There you see, she's with her mother."

It's true, there are some women huddled by the wall not far away. A man stands over them, holding a torch. "And the two boys?" Miriam asks.

She's grateful for the look of pain across his face.

* * *

The women take her to a nearby house, a single long low room divided in the middle with a woolen curtain. The back half is full of women. They sit on the packed earth around the fire. When Judas Sicarius's wife comes in, three women gather up their skirts and rise to greet her. They lead her to a place in the corner where she sits on a stool next to the loom. A small woman not yet twenty, she's too weak to say the words of the lament. She feels her loss too much, Miriam imagines. She sits with her face covered. Her sisters kneel in the dirt around her stool, holding her hands. But one of them, the oldest, stands with a lighted candle in her fist, and it's she who starts murmuring the words they all know, because they've been speaking them or listening to them since they were girls.

Except the words are different every time. The men have their own ceremonies, their own prayers, which they write down and recite. That night they've said their prayers as quickly as they could over the bodies of Judas Sicarius and his sons. They've hurried them underground as quickly as they could, according to the law. At dawn the women will go with flowers to the tomb. But now all night, one after another they'll sing their foolish songs, their lists of deeds and virtues while the rest keen and weep and slap their breasts and murmur wordless chants. Miriam is bored after a few minutes. There's a ringing in her ears. Worse than that, suddenly she remembers her pouch of coins, which she put among the roots of the tree—what did she think? Sicarius is dead, his sons are dead.

They've brought her to a place beside the fire. They've made her sit and pushed a cup of hot water into her hands.

The smoke rises around her toward a hole in the flat roof, but there's a wind that keeps it sealed inside. It spreads out in a layer above her head, and she can feel it in her eyes, her throat. She's thinking about her bag of coins, nestled in a hollow place between two roots. When morning comes, children will find it.

Wordless songs surround her. She wants to get up, go outside, go far away. Judas Sicarius was a good man, good to her. Still, she has no reason to punish herself. What are a few visits, a few drachmae, a glazed pot over the course of years? As for the wife, she met her once before. No, if she gets up now, the women will think she's sick, the smoke has made her sick. Already she's coughing and her eyes are watering. Or if she stands up now, maybe they'll think her eyes are full of tears.

But what does it matter what they think of her? She's the rabbi's mother, after all.

And so she lays down the cup, staggers to her feet, pushes through the curtain. And now she can't stop crying, can't stop her eyes from watering, though she makes no sound. The other side is dark except for one small lamp which shows an empty table, an old man sitting beside it on a stool. His beard is thin and gray, his eyes are stupid and confused. When Miriam looks at him, she imagines he understands nothing of what's happened. Perhaps he can't hear the murmured rise and fall, the women's voices from the other room. There's no grief in his face. His mouth is toothless when he smiles.

Or is he blind? His eyes follow her to the door, but maybe he can hear the sound of her steps. "Stupid old man," she calls him. Then she's out in the cold rain, hurrying down the empty street, her shawl over her head.

Thanks to God, the purse is where she left it. All that coming and going as they pulled the body down under the torches, and nobody saw it. Nobody trod on it. She hefts it in her hand, thrusts it into her belt where she can feel it against her stomach. And she is still kneeling there under the tree beside the broken wall, when her second son comes back to find her. "Woman," he says, "mother, what are you doing here?"

"Murderer. Leave me alone." Her voice is shrill from anger, fear, and she will get up, hurry away, only she slips on the wet ground. Jacob grasps her arm so tightly, she can't pull free. He pulls her to her feet.

"Come," he says. He's pulling her back toward the house, and she can't get away from him. The cold and rain have gone into her joints. Her hands shake. Her clothes are wet. So she's almost relieved to find herself back into the house again, where she can hear the wordless songs behind the curtain. She's standing in the middle of the dark room and the old man sits beside his table.

"Take this off," says her son as he unwinds her shawl. He brings another stool and she slumps down on it. Then he brings a cup of wine. "Drink this and stop your teeth from chattering."

It's unmixed wine from Galilee. "More," she says as soon as she can speak.

He doesn't bring her more. He stands above her with his hand on the table next to the small lamp.

For a moment she's afraid of him. Again she's struck by how much he looks like his brother. They have the same heavy jaw, thick hair, brooding eyes. The same broken nose. In the face only—anyone who knew Jeshua can see it. But Jacob is a small man with narrow shoulders, narrow hips. The small legs of his father, Alpheus the Greek, who took her in when Jeshua was just a baby. No one else would have them. She couldn't forgive him for his ugliness, though she gave him two sons.

Jacob makes a gesture with his hand. He holds his palm out toward her. On the other side of him sits the old man, smiling with his toothless mouth, his empty eyes.

"What have you done?" she asks.

Jacob shrugs and makes the same angry gesture. The lamplight flickers. They listen for a moment to the songs from behind the curtain, the muffled weeping.

"Woman," he says, "I won't let you live like this. Walking the roads like a beggar or a madwoman. Scrounging in the dirt among the ghosts. Living in that house with whores and tribades. This week I'll take you back to Sepphoris."

"They were your brother's friends," she answers, after a pause.

"My brother had no friends except for whores and beggars and adulterers, as the world knows."

Across the table the old man nodded, then shook his head.

She feels the purse of coins in her belt. She's comforted by the weight of it. "My clothes are wet," she says. She smoothes the shawl out in her lap and wipes her face with a corner.

She feels the power of the wine in her heart and head. And her tongue is not in her control. "I'll do what you think best," she says.

Then in a little while, "I'll do what you tell me, because you are my son."

She looks up at him and meets his eyes. "Where you lead me, I will go, and if you make a house for me, then I will live in it."

He shrugs, and she can see he is suspicious. But when she reaches out to touch his hand, he doesn't pull away. He's standing in front of her, his hand on the table beside the empty cup. She takes it in both of hers. "Stay with me," she begs. "Sit with me. Tell me what's happened. I can see it in your face."

He says nothing, and she waits. "I can see your trouble," she repeats.

But he won't talk to her at first, because she's a woman. She looks up at his face, and for the first time she imagines his loneliness. He has no wife, no sons. He's taken up with thieves and liars for the sake of his war against the Romans. Maybe he has no friends among them. Maybe Sicarius was his friend.

She bows her head, and with both her hands she brings his hand up to her forehead. "Sit down here," she says. Rising, she draws him down onto the stool, and then goes to fill a cup of wine for him. The jug is on the shelf, which is set into a corner of the wall. Her hands are aching as she pulls it down.

"No," he says. "No." But she finds a cup and fills it, and puts it down on the table's edge next to his hand. Then she sits in the dirt at his feet.

"Ah, God," he says, finally. "Terrible things are happening."

Then in a little while, "They threw the boys into the cistern," he says. "Sicarius's sons. Oh, mother, these are terrible times."

He grimaces, twists up his face, squints as if a strong light were in his eyes—a habit he's always had, and which she recognizes. What does she feel when looks at him?

His teeth are long and stained. "Saul of Tarsus...," she begins, but he interrupts.

"He's a traitor. He's a spy of the high priest."

"Saul of Tarsus . . . ," she begins again after a moment, because the name seems to make Jacob want to speak. Again he interrupts.

"He's more Greek than Jew. Tomorrow he will eat a meal with the governor. You know the news," though of course she doesn't. No one tells anything to an old woman. "Caligula is dead, and Herod Agrippa will be king in Israel. Already in Jerusalem the crowd is cheering the soldiers wherever they go. Now we will have a Jewish king, according to the prophecies."

Across the table, uncomprehending, the old man yawns. In the lamplight his skin is pale as wax.

Across the table the old man smiles, and Jacob looks up. "Do you understand?" he asks suddenly, as if he's talking to the old man. "Gaius Caligula had a golden statue made with goat's feet and a naked chest, and his own face. He sent it to Caesarea in a special ship with orders for Petronius, the governor of Syria. Bargiona and I were happy, because the people would have risen up—the plans were laid. That was the reason Petronius disobeyed the emperor. Not for the justice of it, but because he was afraid. Then Caligula gave the order for him to be arrested and condemned, but died of the fever before the message was sent. Now the emperor is dead, Petronius is alive, and Herod Agrippa will be king. The crowd throws flowers on the heads of the tenth legion as they march. They say God sent a fever to Caligula to save Petronius's life. Now the new emperor has released Herod from jail, and they say God has blessed him, too. My brother died to chase the Romans out of Israel. Year after year we had a chance, and now the chance is gone."

Across the table the old man shakes his head, then nods. His eyes are rimmed with red. "So Bargiona is with you . . . ," Miriam whispers.

But her son won't let her speak. "Bargiona is a murderer. He lives for money, wine, and fornication, and if he stirs up the people every year, it's not because he hates the Romans. It's the way he keeps his strength. Philip and Andrew, Thaddeus and Simon—they're all murderers. If anyone still wondered, this night proves it."

Miriam listens to the women on the other side of the curtain. Their voices rise and fall. Someone cries out. "What will you do?" she asks.

Jacob shrugs. "I'll go to Galilee and then to Qumran in the desert. I and a few others, we're finished with these fools. But there are men among us who still love the laws of our fathers. Who won't be taken in by this. Herod Agrippa—do they remember nothing? King Herod's grandson. What do they expect out of that family of pigs?"

He's been rubbing his finger against the clay wine cup, touching the shallow bowl, decorated along the outer rim with a green pattern of grapes. Now he takes hold of the stem and drinks. The wine spills into his beard, and he wipes his mouth with the back of his hand. "Where's Bargiona now?" asks Miriam, but he doesn't answer. He sits on the stool, his narrow shoulders hunched.

He doesn't say anything for a long time. She listens to the chanting of the women, and watches him. He's unhappy, and she sees it in the movement of expressions across his face. She rises partway to her knees so she can take his hand. She touches it as gently as she can, a thin weak hand with hair along its back.

He takes another drink, and she watches him grimace in the flickering lamplight. Her own fingers are numb. "I stay in Bethany," she says, "to be near your brother's grave. I know you loved him as I did."

Jacob's face takes on a startled, hunted look. "His grave," he repeats as if confused, but he must know the truth. His younger brothers helped her that night, while he hid with Bargiona and the others. But he must know. "Woman, don't you speak of it," he says, pulling his hand away. "Look what has happened. Bargiona is a murderer. Saul of Tarsus talks to Samaritans, women, uncircumcised Greeks—do you think my brother would have welcomed them and kissed their hands?"

Jeshua spoke to anyone who'd listen, she thinks, but says nothing. Maybe Jacob doesn't remember. Or maybe this is his own kind of loyalty, to imagine Jeshua as a champion of the law.

Jacob is angry now, eager to talk. "If my brother had one thought, it was that a change would come to Israel. Not just that the soldiers would be driven out. But that the wall of the temple would be broken and the sadducees thrown down, and the rich men who torment us, the rich men in their shops. But still the soldiers march through Jerusalem under their pig's head flags, and men like Saul of Tarsus take my brother's words and twist them into reasons to obey Caesar, reasons to do nothing as a new King Herod sleeps in his palace and the high priests count their money. As if the kingdom wasn't here, but in the clouds."

She listens to him almost without breathing. When he's finished, she waits for a few minutes before saying, "You're my son."

She's kneeling in front of him in the dirt. She strokes the back of his hand with her numb fingers and continues, "You have Jeshua's voice. Why have you allowed Bargiona to speak for him?"

Then in a little while, "You were his brother, closer to him than any other."

He twists his lips into an expression of rage. Truthfully, he's not much like Jeshua except in the lines of his face. But he's a better man than Bargiona.

Across the table the toothless old man is nodding and smiling. Can he hear them? Can he understand? His nose is very long, very thin. She can see the bones of his skull under his face. Does he own this house? she thinks. Is he the father of Sicarius, or of Sicarius's wife? Sometimes he sniffs loudly, and Miriam imagines he is smelling the wine, as she is. It's a rich, resinous smell.

"Where's Bargiona now?" she asks.

Jacob grunts and shakes his head. "He's with his brother and a few others. They're hiding from the Romans in a root cellar."

"Where?" she asks.

"In the street of the shoemakers. There are soldiers looking for him all over the lower town, ever since the attack on the embankment and the fire there."

Miriam kneels in the dirt with her head bowed. She's fumbling in the breast of her dress, and in a moment she brings out the small blue pot. She reaches up to place it on the table. "Take it," she murmurs.

But Jacob will say nothing after that. He lurches to his feet, and for several minutes he walks back and forth along the floor. Kneeling in the dirt, head bowed, hands in her lap, Miriam watches him as best she can. "I will stay here with the women," she murmurs finally. "Tomorrow I'll go with you wherever you want, because you are my son."

In her mind she makes an image of four men, squatting around a lantern in the root cellar while the soldiers pass overhead. Their faces are covered. But she imagines she can recognize them: fat Bargiona. Philip and Andrew, who murdered Sapphira of Jericho. Thaddeus the zealot . . .

The rain has stopped. A stream of rainwater has come in past the threshold and made a puddle of mud near the door. After Jacob steps through it to go out, Miriam rises. She has to hold onto the stool at first, because her legs are cramped from kneeling.

There's still wine in the bottom of the cup. "You," she says to the old man. "Do you want this?"

He stares at her, toothless, open-mouthed. But he's not looking into her eyes, which makes her think he's blind after all. "You," says Miriam, and she can see he's trying to speak. He coughs, and then some words come out, creaking and unsure.

"What?" he asks. And then, "What's your name?"

He could mean anything, only she chooses to imagine he might think she's a man. Her voice was always low and harsh. Now she makes it lower, harsher, more clotted still as she pushes her tongue into her sore back tooth, as she says, "Did you hear? Sicarius's murderers are in the street of the shoemakers."

"What?" he says. "What?" His fingers are grasping for the cup, and she slides it across the table. But he knocks it over. The wine smells rich and raw.

Hearing only her voice, maybe he imagines she's a man. She's with him after all, standing beside him. In the other room the women sing and wail. She pours another cup of wine just for herself. Her hands tremble as she lifts the heavy jug.

When the women come out carrying their baskets of flowers, their jars of perfumed oil, she tells them what she's heard. She makes them say the name of the street so they'll remember. Afterward she walks out toward the city of the dead. The women show her Sicarius's tomb. She turns away; she doesn't want to see the bodies laid out. At first light she walks back to her home in Bethany. Her hands are aching, trembling.

CHAPTER FOUR:
THE BLOOD ASCENT

Night after night there was no difference between sleeping and waking, no difference between my dream and what I saw. I woke before dawn and he was there.

In the evening I curled up on my mat of plaited palm, and my doubts came to life around me. Night after night there was an animal, a cave I wandered through, a sea I crossed. No I'm lying—it was not so simple. But I shivered in my blanket, curled up with my bad thoughts, and in the first watch of the night I was breathless, hunted. The care I took to wash myself and oil my thighs and body before I went to bed, in the first part of the night it seemed like crazy vanity. I carried a lump of ice between my breasts. Asleep, I rolled and turned, making noises I could hear because I slept so badly.

How is it that the fire came to me each morning, and each night I forgot? How could my lord have been so patient? Past midnight I would feel the fire burning as the sun rose in me before it rose over the world. Then my bones would unknot and I would stretch out gratefully. The flat rock was as yielding as the couch in my father's house in Magdala when I was just a girl.

My lord would come to me. The fire was in him, yet it never burned me when he rubbed my arms and put his hands under my clothes. He filled me with delight, and I came awake under his hands before I woke into the world. He would speak to me with wise words I couldn't remember, no matter how I tried during the day. But I remembered his rough face, and as the sun came up I would find myself, eyes open, lying on my back, or sitting, or sometimes even standing as the light came through the cracks in the rock. In the middle of a word I would come to myself and stop what I was saying. Because there he was, sometimes naked, sometimes dressed in a red robe fringed with purple. Sometimes he was smiling, or frowning with his finger on his lips. Then every morning I would start to cry, I was so full of my relief. Sometimes I would say, "My love, I dreamt about you, and here you are." Or, "Tell me stories from the land of the dead," though I knew he had spent only three days in that country. Now he was in his father's house. At night he came to visit me, his lonely wife.

He would tell me stories, not with words. He sat by the door of the cave, and I would sit behind him in the shadow. The light cut through the door, and in a jagged patch of light on the red stone he would draw figures in the dust, and they would come alive under his hands. I sat in the shadow with my eyes closed, and in my mind I would watch his big, broken hands, always bleeding from the print of his wounds. I saw the figures in the dust, though I swept the flat stones every day.

In this way I received news of the great world. Once just for a moment I saw the emperor, Gaius Caesar, a white-haired young man vomiting and coughing on his bed, alone in his painted room. Then just for a moment I saw his statue in the shape of the god Dionysus, bare-chested, smiling, with a bunch of grapes in his hand. It was a hot day, and the statue was put up at the dock, and Roman soldiers broke it with their hammers into pieces of dust as the Jews sang and threw flowers.

Or I saw the Roman governor kneel down before the new King Herod in the Xystus, in Jerusalem. He had been freed out of his jail in Rome, and now he came back to his people.

But more often I saw friends I had known, places I had been. I saw the square roof of the house in Bethany where he and I had spent our last hours in each other's company. Its red and yellow walls. Its square courtyard with the sycamore tree. Its barn and stable, empty now of animals. The four women who lived there, Martha and her sister, who were Simon the leper's daughters. The old woman, the mother of my lord. And the black-skinned one whose name I didn't know.

There was a fire in Bethany and soldiers at the well. I saw the woman, Martha, talking to the men who worked for her. Each morning they came out of the desert, or from Ge-hinnon or the villages. Some walked hours to get there. Some she chose, some she sent away according to her need. They worked in the vineyard, the wheat fields, and among the olive trees. At sunset Martha moved among them, and she was dressed in black. Even men who had come for years, she paid them daily with a coin from the purse of her brother Lazarus who owned the land.

I saw the girl, Mary, working in the garden, or at her loom, or grinding flour in the yard. She was smiling, her lips were moving, and I almost heard the music of her song, brought to me out of the valley. Or I saw her with her brother, washing him with a sea sponge, washing his legs, feeding him with a wooden spoon.

I saw my lord's mother up before the light and always moving, always walking, never sitting still. Her clothes dirty and torn, because she slept in them and never changed them. Her gray hair thick and dirty and uncombed, and sprouting now too on her wrinkled cheeks and chin, because she was old. Never quiet, always mumbling and cursing, stalking through Bethany and no one spoke to her.

Once my lord sat on the red stones drawing figures in the dust. He showed me the face of a student of his, a freckled man whose name I didn't remember. But I saw men come to his house in the afternoon. They were carrying torches. Some pulled him from his chair. His legs were swollen and he couldn't walk, so they carried him onto the hill, tied a rope around his neck. They pulled him up into the top of a small tree. He swung back and forth. I recognized Thaddeus the zealot in the crowd, and then some others.

My lord smoothed out the dust with the flat palm of his hand. Then he was writing signs and letters in the Greek alphabet. In my mind I saw his mother climbing down out of a gully in the rocks. It was a place I knew, where the road along the Kidron brook runs through some empty houses. Three boys came from behind a wall and pelted her with stones. The largest boy she knocked down with her fists. But the rest beat her with their sticks until she lay quiet. They found a purse of coins inside her belt.

There was a smell of baked stone all around me that morning, the first day of the passover, I think. I twisted up my hair, squatted over my basin to wash, and then I stood to let the air touch me, God's wind out of the desert through the broken door. There was a smell of dust on my skin, and I was in tears. "God, my God," I said, but could go no farther.

My cave was cut out of the red rock, a small square flat space under a high roof. Light came through a cut window and the broken door. I stood in the patch of light looking out over the valley, the slope of rubble below me and the stair that rose up through it, in places just a few spans wide. Easy to mistake. Below me the stone table where the women left their food, and below that the pool, surrounded now with greenness, because the spring had come. A veil of greenness over the bare rocks.

I turned into my cave, remembering that day six years before, how angry I was. Nor would I stay in the court of gentiles to hear Jeshua speak. But I went to the inner court where I could watch the priests go in and out. What was in my mind? In the temple I received an omen of my husband's death, a voice inside me, and I listened to it. I thought I would be free of him, free of following after him. But that voice lied to me. What have I done but follow him, even since his death?

Now I heard a scratching and a scrabbling in the rocks outside, and I thought it was the rats who came to visit me. God sometimes sent them for my comfort, and they would run from corner to corner of the square room, over the window seat and among my books. I would put out cups of water, crumbs of bread, and laugh to see them. At first they stood up on their hind legs, holding out their trembling paws, and if I made a movement they would scamper away. But in time they grew bolder. When I sat reading or writing they would jump over my legs.

Sometimes I asked myself, why had my husband chosen me? Why had he picked me up out of the dust of the street and put his fingers in my mouth? Why had he chased after me, and married me at Cana at the harvest time? Did he see something in me that I could not see in myself? Did he need me for some task? If so, why did he throw me away?

"I never left you," sometimes he said now at night, in the morning. "But it was you who left."

There was a man in the doorway, hiding his face. "Please," he said, "please," and then I recognized him, Simon Bargiona, whom my husband had called Peter. A man with a big face, and he was carrying two cucumbers in his right hand. He was hiding his eyes, and I went to the window and found an old dress in the pile of clothes. Women brought me clothes now and laid them on the stone table—rich dresses embroidered with their own work, and sometimes I wore them. But that day I dug into the middle of the pile to find the old red shawl, the rags I'd worn six years before.

Peter had his hand in front of his face, shielding his eyes. I let my hair fall over my shoulders, and then I turned to take the cucumbers. "Come, my friend," I said, "sit down. You must be tired."

Without a word he flopped down on my plaited mat. And he was still avoiding me, not looking at me, searching out instead the piles of letters and medallions left on the stone table. Every evening I brought them to my cave—sprigs of painted leather or paper, small pieces of lead, each cut with the seal of a market scribe. Prayers for sick children, mostly.

Or he was looking at my own pots of ink that I used for my writing. "My friend," I said, "I'm glad you've come. There is water in the jar and you see the gourd. I think it will be a hot day."

He was looking at me as if he didn't know my face or remember who I was. After a few minutes I said, "Now you can help me. I was thinking of the time my lord told the story of the woman with ten silver pieces, how she lost one and lit a candle, and searched her house, and when she found it she called to her friends and neighbors—at that time I blamed him, I remember, because I never had ten silver pieces or a house either, all the time I was with him. But now tell me what day it was he told us that. I think we were in Galilee, in Capernaum."

I spoke in the common language, because he knew no Greek. But he shook his head and I wondered, even so, if he understood me. He had not said a word since he came in, and he sat shaking his head, wagging it from side to side. Even though it was one of my fasting days, I found a plate and knife. I cut the cucumber into slices and arranged them in a circle. Then I put one of the slices on my tongue—it was so cool and sweet.

I said, "I was remembering what happened on this day when we were walking to Jerusalem with my lord. Do you remember? He sent you to gather figs from the tree, though it was not the season because of the cold weather. And when you came back empty-handed, he cursed you. Was he joking, do you think?"

Now I saw tears stood in the man's eyes. "My friend," I said, "I have no wish to hurt you."

We sat in silence for a while. Then, "Maybe he was joking," Peter answered. "But the curse still holds. Why do you tell me this? Have you heard the news?"

"I live here. No one comes to visit me."

"The rabbi's brother Jacob threw me out," he said. "He turned the synagogue against me. As for the woman and the silver coins, I remember that day. We were telling him about the men Pilate killed at Golgotha, eighteen men of our brotherhood, all from Galilee. They were captured at the Fountain gate with swords under their clothes, and crucified the morning of the feast, like the rabbi the next year."

Simon Peter had a bald, round head, and a nose with two warts on it. One side of his neck was covered with red spots where the hair from his beard had grown into the skin. "So many of us killed, and I think people will remember Jeshua of Nazareth and no one else. Not the eighteen. Not Dimas and Gestas. Not the thousands when Quinctilius Varus was governor. The bodies stunk for weeks until they rotted and fell down, and I saw clouds of crows on all the hillsides outside Sepphoris in Galilee when I was just a boy. And let me tell you this," he said. "Our brotherhood is ended now, the synagogue destroyed. Philip and the sons of Zebedee were taken in the street of the shoemakers two days ago."

His hands were fleshy, small. "Thaddeus took fifty men across the Jordan into the desert. They escaped. Simon the zealot, a few others. Now the rabbi's brother is in the synagogue house with Bartholomew and Matthew, and the soldiers do nothing against them. Why is that? I wonder."

He had white flecks in the corners of his lips. He sat against the wall, leaning back against the stone. I could see he was tired. "No, but Jeshua of Nazareth will be remembered. For your sake, and for mine, and that pig's ass, Saul of Tarsus. The soldiers found the weapons Ananias bought for us and cleared them out, and now the rabbi's brother is there bowing and praying, making sure no one will walk too far on a sabbath morning."

"He hates the Romans as you do." Then, "Why are you here?" I asked, but he didn't listen.

"I know it was that old whore, the rabbi's mother," he said. "Jacob never would have had the stomach, except for her. Never was a man so cursed with his own family as Jeshua of Nazareth. But she would be surprised to learn how I protected her. Her and those women—do you think anyone would have let them live there year after year, as if they owned the land? Buying and selling and bringing in their grain as if they were men? No, but I kept them safe because I loved her son. The rabbi asked me to watch over them before he died, and I gave him my promise because I loved him."

The words poured out. I thought, men never talk like this to one another. Only to women, and perhaps that's why they hate us. I sat and was quiet, and in time I took another slice of cucumber. I chewed it, and when I swallowed, I could feel the sour knots in my stomach. It was days since I had eaten.

"You didn't come to tell me this," I said.

He grimaced, flinched. "I haven't slept since I escaped. I went back to the house and called for Jacob, but they wouldn't let me in. They kept me in the street. I saw John Mark and his mother and the girl Rhoda. She would have given me food, taken me in—the soldiers were chasing me. But Jacob shut the gate and barred it."

Again I took a slice of cucumber as Peter spoke. "I thought I'd follow Thaddeus across the Jordan, but they've gone too far. All night when I was in prison, I saw their faces, the two boys. As good boys as I'd ever seen. If I hadn't given my life over to this war, I would have liked to have two sons like that."

Then in a little while he said, "Tell me the truth. Have you seen the rabbi since his death?"

"I see him every day," I answered, which was the truth.

"Oh," he said. "Now I can't close my eyes. They had me chained in my cell with no more space than I could lie in by myself. A stone coffin in the dark. I saw those two boys above me, their faces shining with a light. I screamed like a pig, and the soldiers took me out to beat me. Maybe they would have killed me with the others, maybe they were saving me till after the passover, as they said. But they beat me senseless, and when I woke up I was in the street outside in the dark night. Now maybe it was God who set me free, but what I want to know is, did I see God's angel? Or are these spirits come to curse me, follow me to death? No one has come out from the Antonia since Jeshua Barabbas, and he was wounded, maimed. Now I think I have been wounded, and these boys follow me."

I looked down and saw I had emptied the plate. I put my hand over my mouth to hide my chewing. "What boys?" I asked when I could speak.

He looked at me then. "Sicarius's sons. On the day Jeshua of Nazareth was crucified, you know Judas Sicarius betrayed the rest of us. He sold us to the Romans and bought some land with the money. But we escaped and so I let him live, because I imagined that whatever he did, in his own way it was for the rabbi's sake. We were all crazy with unhappiness. I thought God would punish him, and so he did—gave him the dropsy so he could scarcely walk. But then I learned he was conspiring with Thomas Didymus. I had him struck him down in Aceldama so the blood burst from his mouth. But the two boys—Thaddeus and my brother Andrew threw their bodies into the cistern. I saw them floating, their faces swollen. By God, they were just boys, and would have made good soldiers against the Romans."

I thought the cucumber had poisoned me. There was a pain in my stomach, a burning in my throat. I knelt on the rocks. It was hot inside my little cave. The air was hard to breathe. I heard a ringing in my ears, and my tongue was swollen in my mouth. If Bargiona had not been there, I would have drunk all the water in the pot and then vomited it up, purged myself with water when I felt the poison in me. But he was there, sitting next to the clay pot, the gourd beside his hand. Nor had he taken a drop to drink. But he had come in out of the heat of the day. Now the sweat dripped from his forehead, but he wouldn't drink. I heard the scratching of the rats outside the door. I saw the dirt on Bargiona's body, the sweat on his face. My tongue was thick. There was dry air from the desert, but Bargiona had brought a wetness, a closeness to the room. And I saw images of what he had described for me, freed out of the air and given shape. I saw Judas Sicarius, his arms and legs and stomach swollen with disease, so fat and heavy he could barely walk, and he was stumbling in the barren field in Aceldama. The sun burned down on the cracked earth. Under his clothes I could see his man's part full of worms and blood; it hung to his knees. And as I watched, he stumbled down and vomited his life out on the ground, the mass of his body heaving and shuddering.

The more I fasted, the longer I lived by myself in my stone room, the more these visions came to me. But never with such clarity—I saw Simon Peter in his cell in the Antonia fortress, a tiny, cramped space like an oven where he lay full-length. The boys were near him in the dark, tiny presences no bigger than flies. Where they pricked him, they drew blood.

Now he sprawled back against the wall of my cave. "All my life I've tried to live as the rabbi taught us," he muttered. "Now I am old, I feel old," and it was true, he was old before his time. His hair was gone, his forehead ridged and lined, his eyes bloodshot and clouded, his teeth rotten and split. The pores stood open on his nose. His neck was spotted. Only his chest was big and powerful, and the rest of him had shrunken from his chest, as if he were a turtle in its shell. I saw him standing in the street outside the gathering house, a place I'd never been. But I saw its broken-down mud walls, and Jacob of Alpheus standing on the flat roof with the moon above him, the stunted body and the stick in his hand, and the face of his brother lit with a trembling fire from the courtyard, and the smoke twisting up into the clouds. "Go!" he shouted. "Murderer!"

There was only one man born in God's image in the world, and I had married him in Cana and lain with him in the upstairs room, and many times afterward. Pontius Pilate killed him, and he rose from the dead. If he was a man, these others were not men. Still, they were capable of being comforted. Jeshua of Nazareth had touched them, and he was skilled with his hands. He could bring comfort even to lepers, nor did he keep away from them. Once I saw him take a leper in his arms and wash him, and pick the maggots from his sores one at a time, and lay them in a dish of honeyed water. Or I saw him bind up a woman's leg with honey and herbs, and when he took the bandage off the wound was gone. No scar remained. Or I saw him make a plaster out of dregs of wine mixed with a metal dust. Or when I myself was sore with bruises on my feet from the long walks, when we would go back and forth around Lake Tiberias, moving without reason like buzzing flies—we hid from the soldiers in Gergesa, and he washed my feet and touched the blisters with his big hands. At night he talked to us around the fire, and after I had gone off with the women once he came to me and washed my feet with oil, and told me again what he had said, the story of his dream, how he saw two thousand men of the tenth legion falling to their deaths from the rock into the sea where they choked and drowned. The pig's head flag drifted and sank. It was the tenth legion that was burdening the people there in Gadarene.

Peter Bargiona was staring at me now, his eyes unfocused and the sweat glistening on his forehead and behind his ears. I thought, not for the first time, how little these men understood when my lord spoke. That night out of his hearing they had plotted to ambush a small cohort of the tenth—a stupid plan that came to nothing. It was something the men talked about to cheer themselves. But later as my lord rubbed my feet, I didn't tell him I had understood his dream, because that always brought a frown to his face. But I thought I did understand that it was God who would drive the tenth legion out of Israel, and drive out all the legions of devils if we could make a way for him.

This is something women know, that the war takes place inside our bodies. It was something I tried to understand daily in my simple cave among the red rocks, where the dust blew in each day and I swept it out. When I was living there it was my work to purge myself, make myself clean so God would come. And he did come.

The men who followed my lord were too young to give up all their stones and swords and secret talk, the drunken violence they loved. Peter Bargiona was older than the rest, and sometimes in the old days I thought he almost understood. Now I wondered if he had learned something as he was thrown out in the street by Jacob of Alpheus, as he was tortured with the faces of Judas's sons. As I said, he looked old to me, his skin stretched and shrunken, the skin of a fat man who has lost weight suddenly.

As I was thinking this, I saw a shadow pass over the patch of light inside the door. A cloud over the sun, perhaps, but I looked up and saw my lord dressed in purple like the emperor. I saw him put his finger to his lips as he squatted down. And he brought a cool wind with him into that hot, dusty air, which relieved me because all this time I had been suffering with a pain in my stomach, a sick feeling that had risen in my throat. But now I swallowed and it went away. As I watched, he reached out to stroke the bald head of Simon Peter Bargiona, painted with sweat, and I saw the sweat dry under his fingers. He ran his thumbnail over the lines on Peter's forehead. Later the man slumped forward, and my lord laid him out on the palm mat, laid him on his side and made a pillow for his head out of some rolled-up rags I had there.

I looked at my lord's face. There was a soft fire burning behind his skin, which seemed to turn his skin into a membrane that was clouded and unclear, through which I could see his yellow bones. The sight was intolerable to me, so I turned away, and on my hands and knees I crawled into the doorway of my simple cave and sat in the patch of light, and looked out over the valley and the pool below me.

Six years before, Simon Peter had been a powerful man, a good soldier. Among my lord's students there were some who laughed at me and said cruel things. But Simon Peter had protected me. When my lord left me, always Simon Peter would give me some money until they came back, because he kept the purse.

All the time I had sat talking with Peter in the cave, part of my mind was asking the other part why he had come. Three days after his death, I saw my lord standing in the tomb. Afterward I did as he directed me and brought the news to Simon Peter and the others, who were hiding from the soldiers. Thaddeus and Simon the zealot laughed at me, laughed at my tears. But Simon Peter went down on his knees and called me the first of my lord's students. He brought men and women to see me in my cave. Most recently he had brought the woman Sapphira and her husband Ananias.

Now I wondered. Sapphira had carried under her clothes a jar of silver money, and she had given it to me secretly to keep. It still lay on my table. Now as I sat in the patch of light looking out over the valley, I heard a noise like the scratching of the rat. I wondered if Simon Peter had woken up, if he was searching for the silver coins. He was out of sight behind me, but I imagined him looking in all the cracks and fissures of the rock, ignoring what lay in plain sight. I thought there are two Simon Peters, one who believes in Jeshua of Nazareth and in me, the truth of what I saw. And there is one who searches for Sapphira's money.

A mist seemed to rise out of the rocks, and all around me the broken rocks were too hot to touch, though where I sat I felt a cool wind, as I have said. But the dust rose like smoke out of the valley, and the rocks breathed out a shining mist. Light-headed, I felt a ringing in my ears, and heard a sound like the crash of waves on a rock beach. I had not slept the night before, but kept my vigil in the darkness, waiting for my lord. Now I could feel my tiredness, my arms as heavy as sand. It was not possible for me to lift my hands, open my mouth. But I sat dreaming and my thoughts went farther, and I thought there were two Jeshuas, perhaps, and one was the old woman's son from Nazareth, and one was the anointed Christ. One was the man who had found me in the marketplace and married me at Cana. Who had lain with me in the upstairs room, and in rooms and fields and tents all over Israel. Who turned away from me, and only came back when he needed what a woman gives. Who now came to visit me and paw me in my sleep, raising animal desires and doubts no matter how I tried to purge myself and wash my body, scrub my skin.

But I wanted another kind of healing, which was knowledge. The wind came to me out of the desert. It blew to me past all the stews and cities and labors of men and women, the foul smells, the childbirth, the dying animals, the dirt. When it came to me it was full of perfume from the rocks, and I thought the god of all this, who gave the book to Moses, who sent the flood, who demands obedience, who struggles in this chaos with his jealousy and laws and punishment, is not the great God. If he were, then why would he be jealous? But there is a God above him who sent him to rule our bodies as the great God rules our minds. And this great God has a son who is the Christ.

Above me there was not one cloud. The sky was a perfect blue. Below me in the valley the pool shone like a mirror. I saw men and women limping down the path toward it, and a boy leading a donkey. Part of my mind was listening to Simon Peter search among the rocks inside my cave, and I was wondering if he had pretended to sleep so that I would leave him alone. But the other part was rising to the sky, so blue it was almost black. I imagined stars in it, constellations in the shape of letters that would spell out secret words. I imagined the two natures of the great God, one male, one female. In the same way Adam had two natures until the jealous god split him apart.

It is hard to remember my thoughts then, because they mix with my thoughts now, in my tall house in Alexandria, where I write these things down. And I am worthy to do it, because I am first and last, honored and despised, whore and undefiled. I am the virgin and the wife. I am the barren womb, and many are my children. I am shameless and ashamed. At that moment I heard the jar breaking inside my cave, because with part of my mind I had been waiting for it. I heard the jar break and the money spill out. At the same time I heard my lord speak to me, and it was not his rough, remembered voice. But he spoke in a new voice which was not that of my husband, and told me to go to Bethany where an old woman lay dying.

Later, my husband's followers split between his brother and Saul of Tarsus, between the Jews and the Greeks. Bargiona disappeared. I never saw him again. I took only my gray dress and red shawl when I left the valley. I had lived there for years, but now I was eager to be gone. I climbed through the rocks and around the pool, leaving the girls praying undisturbed by the water. And when I was coming down the Blood Ascent to the Jericho road, I met an old woman. She labored toward me out of breath, and when I tried to pass her she put out her hand, took me by the arm. I waited with the shawl around my face while she found the breath to speak. Bent almost double over her stick, she bowed her head, struggling to make a noise. Then she addressed me in the language of the Galileans, asking me if Mary of Magdala lived along this path as she had heard. I pulled the cloth from my face and she peered up at me with a bright, searching look. Then she turned away and tried to spit out of her dry mouth, and made a sign of luck against the evil eye. She was an ignorant peasant after all. Still I told her the truth, that Mary of Magdala had been there but was gone.

In the country of the blind, that woman couldn't recognize the one she looked for. And as I spoke to her, I understood that I would never see again, asleep or awake, the false image of Jeshua of Nazareth bending over me, lying beside me. When he came to me again, I knew I would see him in his true shape.

But first I had to climb once more into Jerusalem. It was my test, to take leave of those women. And so I covered up my face and came to Bethany in the hot afternoon, with only a few hours on the road. Though I felt weak, I knew I could have nothing to eat or drink. Nor could I stop to make water or make dirt, though I could feel the air inside of me pushing out. When I came to the hill of Olives, I thought I must climb up and rest under the trees. But instead I turned down by the well.

Soldiers of the tenth legion were there, and the centurion on his black horse. He had a red sash tied across his body. His hand was in the air, and he was trying to shout over the noise. His hand moved as the big horse bowed and pranced. Ten soldiers were with him, and one carried the banner of the red pig. The rest held up their square shields, because there was a screaming and boys were throwing stones. I heard the crack of the stones. Bethany was a village of no more than thirty houses, and some of these boys must have come from elsewhere, I was sure. But there was always trouble here, the grinding of enemies. Houses had burned down.

A smell was rising up behind me from a crevice in the rocks, a place where men came to squat. I didn't want to show myself, so I waited until the smell no longer seemed foul to me. I waited until I was no longer afraid. Then I stepped down into the edge of the crowd. The boys had fallen back. The men made a path for me as I ran. I had my shawl over my face and I was weeping, because I was remembering the day six years before when Jeshua of Nazareth came back to Bethany along that road. The next day Peter Bargiona attacked the soldiers at the temple, and everything was done.

I ran down the street until I could no longer hear the noise. I passed a broken cart. Then I came in under the stone gate and saw the sycamore tree, its leaves green and new.

The house was closed, but as I stood under the tree looking up at its strong branches, the girl came to me, tears in her eyes. She kissed my hands, pressed my hands against her forehead, and I could feel her tears against my skin.

"Come quickly," she said.

She was small, with wide black eyes. Her face was uncovered, her black hair loose over her shoulders. She wore a piece of frayed red string around her neck. Knotted into it were two glass beads. When she bent over my hands, I saw a scar at the base of her neck. Her own hands were rough and scarred.

"Come," she said, pulling me toward the house. "The men are fighting. How did you get here?"

But there was no reason to answer any questions. It was not why I had come. "Where is she?" I asked. I knew she was not dead.

I was looking for the woman who gave life to my husband, Jeshua of Nazareth, because I knew she was in pain. When the mother of all creatures was delivered of the world, she found it deformed by her own suffering. There is a piece of the great God in each of us, if we can find it and hold it in our hands.

As I crossed the courtyard under the sycamore tree, I looked up into its green and yellow leaves. I felt that I held a treasure in my cupped hands, and it was seeping out between my fingers. Now I know what I know, but in those days it was still fresh. I felt I had dreamed the world. Awake, I labored to remember what I'd dreamed.

"Where is she?" I cried.

So the girl brought me into the first room, where Jeshua's mother lay on a bed. It was a dark place, low- ceilinged, and the old woman was curled up around her wounds. She lay on her side on the low pallet with the blanket over her.

All day it had been overcast, but now the sun came out. I could feel it even from inside the house. There was a window with a wooden shutter, and needles of light pierced through it without lessening the darkness, which overwhelmed the tiny candle by the bed. As I knelt down I felt the sunlight pressing on the flat roof. I saw the two other women sitting at the foot of the bed, Martha of Bethany and her servant, Sarah.

I closed my eyes, and when I opened them all three of them were sitting there, the two sisters and the black Egyptian. Their faces had neither questions nor answers. They wanted nothing, nor expected anything. They were content to sit and wait for the old woman to die. Or else they were not content, because the girl was crying. Yet she sat calmly, her cheeks wet with tears. She wore a gray dress with patched sleeves, and she had a red string around her neck. The glass beads glinted in the candle light, and I saw the streaks of her tears. She had a small chin, a small mouth and a flat nose, all of which made her eyes seem large, her forehead wide and smooth. As I watched, she gathered her hair behind the nape of her neck, and fastened it quickly and neatly with a metal pin.

Her sister sat beside her, taller and bigger, with wide shoulders. She was wearing a black dress which was embroidered around the neck in a pattern of flowers. She had a belt of twisted chains. She had a ring in each ear and several on each hand. She had a bracelet on her wrist. Her hair was coarse and rough, cut short as if in mourning. She had a strong, straight nose and heavy eyebrows, a sign of beauty among the Greeks. Her eyes were lined with a dark powder, and her lips were painted red, a dark cherry color against her skin.

Then there was the Egyptian, younger, I thought, than either of the others. She didn't look at me. I saw the side of her face only, the outline of her nose, the white gleam of her eye. Her hair was hidden under a ragged cloth twisted around her head. Her dark lips were parted, and I could see the line of her teeth. Her head was small, her neck long and naked, and she wore a bleached woolen shawl over her shoulders. I could see her hands restless on her knees. As I watched, she reached out with her long forefinger and touched the bracelet around Martha's wrist, a heavy silver cuff.

There was a beeswax candle set on an iron spike and a pan to catch the drips. I knelt down in the dirt and stretched my hand over the old woman's head. Under the ragged blanket I could see her fine gray hair, her delicate and spotted cheek. She was sleeping, and her breath was light.

"Don't disturb her," Martha said. But I had to. She could not lie there with her breath softer and softer until she slipped away. To die in darkness is the worst thing. I put my hand on her thin shoulder and shook her awake, gently at first and then more violently.

A low groaning came out of her, a rustling in the straw. I pushed her over onto her back. "Wake up," I said and would have told her to listen. I would have told her not to let death take her while she slept. I would have told her to bring Christ to the center of her mind, so that he could make a bridge for her out of the world. I would have told her to hold fast to his name and repeat it every moment. That would have been my gift to her, even after all her cruelty. I shook her by the shoulder, and Martha rose to stop me. But then she hesitated, because the old woman woke up. Her old eyes opened, and they were glittering and clear. I bent over her and smelled her breath, which was already that of a corpse. I saw her spotted cheeks, her long nose and upper lip. Hair sprouted from a mole in the corner of her mouth.

Her voice, when it came, was firm and clear. She didn't scream or shout. She did not whisper or mutter. "You crazy, stupid whore," she said. "You keep away from me."

I wanted to tell her about the city of light where the streets are laid out in a simple pattern. But when I bent down to whisper the name of the great God, she pushed me away, blocking my mouth with her old hand.

CHAPTER FIVE:
MARTHA'S TREE

After three years, Thaddeus the zealot comes out of the desert with two hundred men. They march from Jericho. But the soldiers stop them on the hill of Olives.

He's displayed before the crowd at the Antonia, and Martha's sister asks if she can go and see. So Martha tells Jonathan to accompany her. He is a man who has been with them since their father's death.

Now Martha speaks to Mary in the dark house. "Take these things. Go to the Xystus and have him wait outside the shop. You know the one. You've been there before. The shopkeeper will recognize the bracelet. Do not accept less than—" and she names the price. "If he offers less, sell him this and this and bring the chain back with you."

When she fetches a basket, Martha says, "No. Hold them in your belt. Don't carry anything with you, not even a loaf of bread. Keep to the roads. People are hungry in Ge-hinnon."

"But you wear this every day," says Mary, holding up the ring that Sarah made.

"Yes, you're right." It's just that Martha wants it to be gone. "Take it. And let me show you something, in case anything should happen."

She brings her to the hearth, pries up the stone. "This was Simon the leper's place."

Martha reaches into the crack beneath the biggest stone and draws out the old leather bag. Once it was full of gold and silver coins. But nine years is a long time. There are only a few left. She opens the long neck of the bag and drops in the belt of silver chains, the gold chain from around her neck. She wants them to be safe.

What is Mary thinking now? Martha ties up the leather bag and thrusts it beneath the stone. She puts the hearthstone into its slot. After Simon the leper's death, his cousin searched for this place. He had an idea it wasn't in the house. He dug up the courtyard and the floor of the barn, then found the iron box that Sarah had hidden under the roots of the sycamore tree. The box held some of the gold coins, enough to satisfy him.

Martha and her sister have never spoken of these things. Now Martha looks up at Mary's face, where she kneels holding the lamp. She is staring at Martha's hands as she smoothes the dirt over the stone.

"Let's go," Martha says. She gets up, brushes off her knees. Then they go out into the bright heat of the day. There has been no rain for months.

They walk under the sycamore tree. Its leaves are brown and brittle. There is a branch that sticks out from the trunk. Martha reaches up but cannot touch it.

Jonathan waits at the stone gate. "You keep her safe," Martha says and he nods his head. He is simple in his mind. He's a small man with a limping walk.

First she thinks she will say goodbye to Mary there at the gate. But then she walks on farther down the street, past the burned houses that have never been rebuilt. They say nothing as they pass the well. When they reach the olive trees, Martha stops. Lazarus is in the house, and thieves might come. Already this is farther than she has ever been outside the town.

Martha stands under the dusty trees and watches Mary go. She's gone over all of this in her mind, yet it still hurts. She watches the man limp out of sight, and then she returns home. Along the way she stops beside a wheat field that once belonged to her. Anyway, nothing grew this year.

Inside the gate she turns and stands in the place where she stood waiting the night Simon the leper died. It was the same night they brought Jeshua of Nazareth from Golgotha and put him in the tomb. She stood here and put her hand on this gray stone, and watched a shape loom out of the darkness, Sarapias, Isara's daughter, carrying a basket.

Now Martha can't remember the look of her face or what she was wearing. She is confused by other memories. The image of the woman has supplanted the girl, as the known has supplanted the unknown. Nor was the color of her skin remarkable. Martha had seen Jews just as dark. But perhaps her hair wasn't visible. Perhaps it was tied in a white cloth, which was her custom later.

How strange it is, Martha thinks, that you can see someone every day, be with them every day, and when they're gone, nothing remains. Or what remains is just a handful of thoughts and pictures in the mind. Sarah walked across the courtyard thousands of times and left no mark.

Or perhaps it's the way Martha is, what she's become, that is the trace left behind. Once on the hillside there stood two olive trees, planted close together. One developed a disease and was cut down. But it was still there in the way the other one was twisted out of shape, changed from what it might have been.

"I was born when Venus was just rising in the east. It was the morning star. Saturn and Mercury were in the seventh house. I know what I am," Sarah told her once, meaning that she had seen the chart in her father's house, in Egypt. She had broken into the chest beside his bed.

"It could have been the same for you," she'd said.

"It could have been," Martha replied.

You must look deeper to find the trace, Martha thinks now, standing by the gate post. There are small things. She goes in search of them. In the ash heap by the corner of the barn there are slivers of a plate that Sarah broke. And what about the scratches on this piece of stone here by the garden wall? She had made the sign of the new moon one lazy night when all the others were asleep.

Thaddeus the zealot was taken on the hill. Most of his men were killed and he was wounded. After the fight, the soldiers had come down to the well at Bethany to water their horses, because the Kidron brook was dry.

Five soldiers had come through the town, beating a drum and calling out the people. Most of the men had run away, but the boys were there. Some of the women had gone out to see. Martha's sister had pulled her by the hand, but when they came to the bottom of the street, she had hung back. The women and boys stood quietly, and in the gap Martha had seen Thaddeus the zealot standing upright with his hands tied in front of him. There was blood and dirt on his face. As she watched, one of the soldiers gave him some water from his helmet.

Thaddeus was a brave man. When he had drunk, he spat the water in the soldier's face. Even then he struggled to get away. But the soldiers kicked him down and beat him with a stick. Mary was crying. When Martha put her arms around her and covered her face, she could still feel the beating of the stick as if it struck her sister's body. She put her cheek against Mary's head. Above them in the rocks over the well, she saw the flags, the golden eagle and the boar's head of the tenth legion.

But as they were coming home, the women's anger turned against them. Their house was the last one, the finest in the town. Simon the leper had built it out of stone. Mary was crying all the way as they came up toward the gate, and Martha had her arms around her. But there was a noise in the crowd, which had been silent until the soldiers marched away. Women stumbled against them. Some of the boys were throwing stones and clumps of earth. A stone struck her behind the ear so that her ear swelled up.

Now she stands in the dry bean field and looks south toward the stable. That was where Jeshua of Nazareth stayed before he went into the city for the last time. But the mud walls are charred and broken. Four months ago, someone lit the roof on fire.

She hears a noise from the house, a high wail. As she turns, she feels the ridges of dry dirt crumble to dust under her toes. The dirt is hot under her feet. She wishes the sound would stop and never come again. Apart from that she feels no urgency. It is a matter of turning her brother over as he lies in bed. The sores on his buttocks give him pain.

She will do these tasks once more and that's the end.

But as she walks toward the house, the wailing stops. It is replaced by a low cough, which will sometimes last for hours. She stands in the kitchen yard for a few moments, looking at her brother's window. To her right is the thatched shelter with the kitchen fire and the grinding stone, the big earthenware pots, and on the far side the washing room and the women's door into the house. But she turns the other way and walks between the wall and the barn into the courtyard.

Simon the leper built this house of stone blocks set with mortar, caulked and washed with ochre-colored clay. The flat roof is a good one, repaired each year with wicker, mud, and straw, and then loaded with bundles of dried brush. Simon the leper built the arch of the gate, and planted the sycamore tree. As Martha passes under it, she reaches up to try and touch the low branch, but cannot.

She steps over the stone threshold into the big room that runs the width of the house. It is dark and stuffy, and the hearth is cold. She makes a circuit of the walls, touching the benches and her father's wooden chair, as if for the last time. She stands for a moment over the place where Sarah had slept beside the hearth stone. All the time she's listening to her brother's cough.

Beyond the big room are two inner rooms, and Martha pushes through the curtain on the right hand side. The shutter is open and the room is full of light. Her brother lies on the bed near the window. Martha stands watching him for several minutes. His coughing has subsided, and she hears a low, steady groan. He has turned onto his side.

Mary fed and changed him before she left. Now Martha comes and sits beside him. She looks down on his withered face, his pale beard. His eyes are closed. The hair of his beard is as soft as the hair on a man's head. He is thirty-one years old.

As she sits, she raises her hand above his face and imagines what would happen if she brought it down over his nose and shrunken lips. Not for the first time, she imagines sealing his mouth and nostrils with her palm. Would his eyes start open? Would some strength come back to him so that he could pull away? Would he bite her fingers with his long brittle teeth?

There was a time when she took pleasure in hurting him, but not any more. Sometimes she had pinched him hard enough to raise a bruise, had scratched his ankles and behind his ears until he bled. This was especially true when their father was alive, because Simon the leper used to come into this room. He used to sit and weep where she is sitting now.

Now she wonders what their lives would have been like, if not for the accident. Her sister would have moved away into another man's house. Lazarus would have married and brought his wife here. Perhaps there would have been children, and Martha would have cared for them.

When her mother died, Simon the leper was too crippled to marry a third time. Instead he gave her to a woman's work, though she was eight years old.

She finds herself combing Lazarus's hair between her fingers, examining it for lice. The lice and flies are terrible this spring.

He moves under her hands, falls over onto his back. His eyes are open now, and as always she is surprised by how little they have changed. His face shows the bones of his skull. His gums have pulled back so that she can see the black roots of his teeth. But his eyes are the same. Almost she can imagine he must have some understanding left, because he looks at her in the embarrassed way he did when she was young, and he decided he could not protect her from Simon the leper. God punished him for that, she thinks. Or perhaps it is the reason he attacked the soldier Cleopas at the well. He could not bear to see his other sister touched, after what had happened.

Now he looks at her with his black eyes. She can almost imagine he's about to speak. Perhaps he knows what she intends. Or perhaps when he sees her face, then he remembers something, some wisp of a vision of when they were children and their mother was alive. She herself cannot remember, but he was older.

She's sitting with his head on her lap, combing his hair between her fingers. His mouth is open, and she smells his bitter breath. Then she can't look at him anymore. She pushes him away, stands up, and he rolls over onto his side.

Martha hasn't been inside many of the houses in Bethany. But she knows how they are built: four rooms around a square courtyard. This house is different. The courtyard is in front, the store room and the barn are away from the house, and all these rooms inside are joined. Now she ducks under the lintel and enters the airless, windowless, small room where Sapphira of Jericho died three years before. There's a lamp burning on the floor, and she picks it up. Then she pushes through the curtain into the corner room. The ceiling is so low she has to stoop. There's a pallet of rushes on the dirt floor, a tangled knot of linen in the middle of it. A crutch stands in the corner of the wall. This is where Simon the leper used to sleep.

She has not come here for nine years. Sarah used to hook back the woolen curtain and ask her to go in. "There's no one," she'd say. But Martha always had refused. Now she stands looking at the tiny, dusty place. She remembers the sound of her father's crutch upon the floor. She holds the lamp above her head.

Next she goes into the place where her sister sleeps alone now. Beyond it is the door to the kitchen garden. The floor is tiled there next to the washing room. One tile has a crack.

Light comes through the open door. She pinches the lamp's wick between her fingers and sets it down. Immediately she smells the smoke. Then she kneels in front of the chest where she and Mary keep their clothes. At the bottom, she finds a dress of fine bleached wool.

There are two washing rooms, one for the men, open to the yard. But the women's room is inside the house. It has a wooden door which is open now. There is a drain set in the tiles.

She filled the big jar from the cistern the day before. Except for her brother there is no one in the house. She stands up, strips off her dress and then her linen clothes. At the same time she is wrapping a linen sheet around herself. Then she ducks her head to step through the door into the little room. She squats down over the drain, and with the dried shell of a gourd she dips out water from the jar onto her hair and shoulders. There is a small pot of oil, which she uses to wash herself under the wet sheet.

The memory of Sarah does not leave her. Nor the memory of the night her father died.

* * *

It was sunset, and the sky was bruised over the hill of Olives. Martha went out to the storage room beside the barn. Her brother Lazarus heard the noise when he was lying on his bed. The chain hurt his ankle, but he got up and went to stand at the window. He stood looking out over the bean field. He couldn't speak and couldn't go to her, but he stood at the window with his hands on the sill. Then he knelt down and put his cheek against the wall. His body was too heavy for his strength. There was not a sound from the courtyard or the animals in the barn. That day he had heard his father limping through the house, but now all was quiet.

In that village of thirty houses near the east wall of Jerusalem, in the days before the feast, Roman soldiers were seen upon the hill, because of the disturbance in the Temple. That night Lazarus heard nothing from the town, even though it was the hour when men return from working and the sabbath lamps are lit behind the curtains. Lazarus tried to speak. He felt spit on his chin. Then he was quiet again, so he could listen to the soft sound of weeping across the yard.

When it was dark, Martha came back with a wooden bucket, and she filled it at the cistern. She washed her hands and face in the water, and then she carried the bucket down behind the barn again.

She moved quickly until she was out of sight of the main house. Then she limped down through the kitchen garden behind the barn until she came to the storage shed, which was built between the barn and the outside wall. She hesitated at the wooden door, unlocked, open, and the lamp was inside. There was the palm mat where her sister Mary was forced to sleep after the soldier touched her. Simon the leper had forbidden her the house, had laid out this bed for her between the big clay jars.

Now it was Martha's place of shame. Now she squatted down. She had chosen this place in the crisis of her illness, on the night when Jeshua of Nazareth was taken by the Romans. And the blood had come out of her, and the small lifeless thing. She had tied it in a strip of cloth torn from her clothes. She had placed it in behind the jars where it still lay. Now she dragged the bucket across the threshold, and with her cupped hands she poured water over the mat, trying to wash it out once more.

Every few hours for these few days, Martha had gone to the place behind the wine jars. Now she put down her bucket, and with a stick she poked at the tiny bundle of rags. Now on the night of the rabbi's death, she was there with the stick in her hand, ringing the lip of one of the big jars. Then she threw it down, and squatted down, and put her hands over her broad, flat, swollen face.

Her brother heard the stick against the jar, and her father heard it too. He limped down through the bean field, leaning on his crutch, and Lazarus watched him through the window. The air smelled of smoke. Lazarus reached down and scratched at the leather cuff around his ankle where the chain ran through. Then he lay down on his stomach on the bed, while his father passed the corner of the barn. He was carrying a lantern, holding it up as he came to the door of the shed. He stood for a moment with the lantern swinging back and forth, and then he put it down inside the threshold on the dirt floor. But there was another lamp inside, and he could see his daughter squatting among the jars. He came to her, knelt, and put his arms around her shoulders, weeping, as he often did since Martha's mother died. She wouldn't look at him, even after he pulled her hands away from her face. Instead she stared into a corner of the room, and after a moment he followed her eyes, looked where she was looking. The shadows were deep around the jars, the bags of grain. But then he saw it. He reached out with the end of his crutch to turn over the blood-striped pouch of rags. "How many days?" he whispered. Then he stood up, frightened now, his face frightened and angry.

* * *

When Martha needed help, Sarah had come. When she was standing inside the gate with her hand on the gray stone, when she was staring out into the darkness, when she was thinking she would walk out into the dark and leave that house forever, then Sarah came to her. She had a white cloth around her hair. And though she was just a girl, a runaway slave, still she knew everything that must be done.

Paul of Tarsus is a great man now. He wrote a letter that is read in the synagogues. "God gives them to degrading love. Their women exchange nature for what is unnatural. They are filled with evil and idolatry, which is also known in Egypt." The next night, men set the stable roof on fire.

"Come with me." But Martha swore she could not leave her sister, her brother, or this house. That was a lie, for as she washes herself, Martha imagines she will leave them now, for good and always. What is the truth? Perhaps only she is not the kind of woman who could cross the sea. Where would they live, what would they use for money? She has never been as far as the gates of Jerusalem. She is the faithless one. She can't live among the gentiles like the rabbi's wife, who is a whore now in the streets of Alexandria, a rich woman, or so men say.

"Come with me. Believe in me." But she could not. Sarah had gone alone, dressed as a man.

Now Martha gets up. She rubs her hair with a dry cloth. She rubs her shoulders and arms, and then puts on the new bleached woolen dress over her new linen underclothes. She dresses like a bride at the feast, then leaves the wet sheet in a clump on the tiles. She walks out the door into the sun. The dust sticks to the soles of her feet.

For many nights Martha has sat up in the big room, or else gone out with a lamp into the dark courtyard. She has thought about what she would say. She's imagined how Sarah might come in through the gate, broken and punished. Perhaps, she thinks now, the men caught her and beat her at the edge of the town, or in Jerusalem, or Gaza.

Purposeful, Martha walks across the kitchen garden to the store room. On the way she turns into the courtyard to stand under the sycamore tree, dry now in the drought. She reaches up to touch the jutting branch.

She has the wooden key in her hand. When she comes to the store room, she slips it into the slot and pushes open the door. Along the wall are shovels and old pieces of rope, and the small barrel she will need. There are the empty wine jars, and at the end, the straw mat where her sister used to sleep years before. She doesn't need to step inside and see. But she remembers squatting there and crying until her baby came out.

* * *

The night Jeshua of Nazareth died, Sarah Sarapias came to Bethany with a message. She found the house of Simon the leper, which was as the old woman described it, the largest in the village, a stone house behind a wall at the end of the street. Its flat roof was loaded with bundles of dried brush. Sarah the Egyptian stepped under the arch of the gate into the courtyard and stood under the sycamore tree, the barn in front of her, the house on her left hand. There was not a sound except the donkey snuffling in its pen.

She stepped through the open door into the house. She stood beside the hearth which glowed with coals. A light burned behind the curtain of the inside room. She pulled it back and peered inside, and saw a naked man sleeping on his stomach on the low bed.

Then she came out into the yard again and a woman was there, the one Miriam of Nazareth described. "I have a message for your father," Sarah said.

But the woman didn't look at her. She was standing underneath the tree, staring out the gate. With one hand she clutched a bundle in the breast of her dress. "My father is dead," she murmured, calmly.

Later she led Sarah down behind the barn. Trouble brought a closeness, and they hardly spoke. But Martha picked up the lantern and stood in the doorway, while Sarah went inside the shed.

Then there was a silence until Sarah broke it. "Miriam of Nazareth sends her compliments, because she is bringing the body of her son. She will be here before dawn."

"My father won't allow it." Martha's face kept no expression. She stood with one hand clutched at her breast. The other held the lantern on its chain. "He fell and hit his head," she continued, though it was she who had the wound over her eye.

"His legs were weak," she continued. "He put his hands to his heart and then he fell. He cried out. But I could do nothing."

Sarah squatted down next to the body, which lay twisted where it had fallen over a bag of barley. The old man lay on his back. His neck hung down. His face was in the light—flat, beardless, smooth, the same face as his daughter's. There was not a mark on him, although his crutch was broken.

"Does he have brothers here?" asked Sarah, and the woman shook her head.

"Is there someone from the village . . . ?" Sarah asked.

Martha stood expressionless with the lantern at her feet. Both hands clutched her tiny bundle, and she pushed it down into her clothes. Then she stepped outside into the darkness. When she came back, her hands were empty.

Later Sarah searched behind the barn. She took the child into the bean field that same night. She said a prayer to Hermes, God of the dead, and buried it among the hummocks and small plants.

But Martha said a different prayer over her father's body. She lit candles at his head and feet. She stretched the old man out on the dirt floor, arranged his withered limbs. Sarah came out of the darkness, wiping her hands. She sat down beside the door.

Mary arrived during the second watch, the younger sister, Cleopas's wife, who had been at Golgotha. She stood on the threshold, and Sarah heard her quick, hissing breath. She stepped over the threshold and came forward.

Her breath came hissing out. Then her face crumpled with tears as she came to sit. Her hands were busy with her father's clothes. She touched her father's clothes, put her hands out to his face, but she wouldn't speak of him. In time the words rose out of her, hindered by tears and her quick breath.

It was as if she spoke a hidden language. The words were covered up with weeping, but then finally they showed themselves. "The rabbi's mother bought a tomb in Aceldama—she won't use it now. The soldiers took the woman of Magdala as she was climbing down."

"You be quiet," Martha said. "Be quiet now."

Mary tried to obey her; she tried to swallow the words. But she was too frightened not to speak. The high-pitched words came out: "My lord died in the sixth hour. The soldiers put his eye out and nailed him to the crossbar. When it was dark, his brothers pulled his body down and put it in the barrow. I ran all the way from Kidron. I thought I'd see his ghost."

Sarah got up and slipped away into the darkness. She heard Martha's voice. "Be quiet now."

"I will, I will," said Mary. And she did try. But then: "Now the rabbi's mother is coming here. I told her we could put my lord in Lazarus's tomb. I didn't think I . . . "

Then for a moment she couldn't speak, because the sobs shook her.

She knelt down, whispering and crying. She reached her hands out toward her father's face. "What will becomes of us?" she asked, but Martha didn't answer. She sat in the shadows, pressing the hot parts of her face with the fingertips of her left hand. Then she was staring out the wooden door into the darkness, until Mary said: "That black girl is from Egypt. Now she's with the rabbi's mother. I don't know. The Romans took Mary of Magdala on the hill. Will they beat her?"

Martha listened to her sister's breath grow calm, and watched her tears dry as she knelt over Simon the leper's head. "What will become of us?" she said again.

Then suddenly there was a sound of dogs barking in the street on the other side of the stone wall. There was the creak of a wooden wheel. At the same time the women heard a screaming and a crying from their brother Lazarus. They ran through the field and saw him at the window, hammering his hands on the sill. Sarah joined them when they crossed into the yard, and under the pink sky they saw two men pushing a heavy wheelbarrow through the gate. Miriam of Nazareth stood under the sycamore tree, and she shook her fist. "Make him stop," she said, half in a whisper. But as she spoke, then Lazarus was quiet as if she'd choked him suddenly with a hand over his mouth, and the dogs stopped barking too.

* * *

Now Martha turns again into the light and stands up straight. She walks across the bean field, the rope curled in her hand. It will be hours until Mary comes back. So in the heat of the day she walks across the bean field to the bottom of the garden, to the rabbi's tomb. There is a stone bench where his mother used to sit. Now she sits there too.

What was it Sarah said? "Come with me—no. You stay here because the charlatan is here, the magician with no magic. You saw them put him in the tomb. A year later you helped seal him in the box. No man was deader."

And perhaps Sarah was right about both things. But there is something comforting about the place. At that moment the truth would not console her. Nor would she take comfort in the knowledge that the branch will break with the rope over it, and she will forget about the Egyptian, and will live in that house with her sister until they are old women and Jerusalem falls. She puts her palm on the warm stone of the seat. She remembers the rabbi's mother and the rabbi too, whom she had loved when she was young. She thought he might heal Lazarus and all the others, all the sick men, the blind, the lame. She'd heard stories of such miracles. Once she came out to this garden and stood there by the cistern with a bucket in her hand, and watched him and Lazarus playing with her sister when Mary was just a little girl. They were throwing her back and forth between them, and she was laughing and squealing.

Printed in the United States
1507500001B/67-84